TAN

Eighteen months after they had separated, Kathryn learned that her husband Cesare had lost his memory after an accident—and his family were suggesting that if they met again the sight of her might bring his memory back. But wasn't it far more likely that Cesare would also remember what had wrecked their marriage in the first place?

TANGLED SHADOWS

BY

FLORA KIDD

MILLS & BOON LIMITED
17–19 FOLEY STREET
LONDON W1A 1DR

First published 1979
Australian copyright 1979
Philippine copyright 1979
This edition 1979

© Flora Kidd 1979

ISBN 0 263 73127 8

Set in Linotype Pilgrim 10 on 12 pt.

*Made and printed in Great Britain by
Richard Clay (The Chaucer Press), Ltd., Bungay, Suffolk*

CHAPTER ONE

FOR the fourth morning that week Kathryn felt nauseous when she sat down to breakfast in the sun-bright ultra-contemporary kitchen of the villa known as L'Hermitage, which was perched on a rocky cliff overlooking the glittering blue expanse of the Mediterranean Sea.

'I'm sorry, Daisy. I can't eat anything,' she sighed. 'Just to look at that omelette makes me feel ill.'

'Humph! What's got into you? It's not often you're off your food.' Daisy Hardcastle's face, pale and plump like a suet dumpling beneath a frizz of grey hair, expressed disapproval. 'You haven't even drunk your tea. Why don't you drink it up? A good strong cuppa in the morning always makes me feel better when I've got a touch of indigestion or if I've been out on the tiles the night before.' Her blue eyes quizzed Kathryn in a kindly way. 'You and Constance were late getting back from that party last night. Did you have a good time?'

'I suppose so,' Kathryn shrugged indifferently. 'But I didn't have too much to drink, if that's what you're thinking is wrong with me.' She rose to her feet. 'I don't want the tea either.'

'Then how about coffee?'

'*Ugh!*' Kathryn shuddered. 'The thought of it makes me feel sick,' she whispered, pressing her fingers against her stomach.

'If you asked me ... which you haven't ... and if I didn't know you're good, clean-living lass who doesn't go sleeping around with any Tom, Dick or Harry, I'd say you were suffering from morning sickness. And you know what that means, don't you?' said Daisy severely.

'Yes, I know what that means,' muttered Kathryn, and went from the room.

Daisy didn't miss much, she thought as she wandered through the spacious elegant lounge of the villa and out on the terrace. And the housekeeper had guessed correctly: it was morning sickness she was suffering from.

Strolling over to the lounger, she sat down on it, swung her legs up and gazed out at reddish rocks and dark green cypress trees sloping away below the terrace to the shimmering blue of the sea. She leaned back and closed her eyes. If she rested for a while the nausea would pass, she knew from past experience.

Eleven whole weeks had gone by since she had walked out on to this terrace and had seen Luigi sitting with Constance at the table under the striped umbrella. How clearly she could remember everything that had happened that day in May when the trees and flowers, now so dusty and full-blown, had been freshly green with new shoots and buds, when springtime had been in full swing.

There had been nothing unusual about the beginning of that day, nothing to warn her that a change was about to come into her life. After breakfast she had driven into Monte Carlo to do some shopping for Constance and Daisy and afterwards, on sudden impulse, she had walked up to the Royal Palace.

Even now against the darkness of her eyelids she could imagine the pale stone gleaming in the sunlight and the square towers with their battlements. It was an enchanting story-book palace, a perfect background for the daily ceremony of the changing of the guard which she had gone to watch. Even now she could hear the roll of the drums, the blare of bugles. It was all so clear in her mind, every detail of what had happened that day, and she felt as if she were reliving it all over again. . . .

Her eyes shaded by sunglasses against the glare of sunlight on the pale walls of the castle, Kathryn stood with several hundred other people, most of them tourists, to watch with fascination the pageantry and precision of the performance. She had been living in Monaco for over a year, yet she could still be delighted by the age-old ceremony which recalled the past of the Principality.

The returning guards marched away, shoulders straight, legs moving in unison, bright buttons and polished shoes glinting in the spring sunlight, and from the highest battlemented tower of the palace the chimes of a clock tolled the hour of noon. The ceremony was over, and so were her few hours of leisure.

She turned away from the palace and made her way down a narrow winding alley past tiny souvenir shops where ashtrays and mugs were displayed, each one depicting Prince Rainier and Princess Grace exchanging fond glances. Between the terraces of buildings climbing the hillside she could see the sea flashing blue and silver and had a view of the harbour where yachts of all sorts and sizes nestled against the pontoons of the marina or swung aloof at moorings.

At last she reached a square, ablaze with flower beds and shaded by palm trees, in front of the nineteenth-century building of the famous Casino where she had parked the small British car belonging to Constance Dale, her employer. Dodging through the traffic, she crossed to a café and took a seat at one of the outdoor tables. There

was time for her to have lunch in that busy place which
provided quick snacks, day and night, to suit all tastes,
before she drove back to L'Hermitage, the villa owned by
Constance, who was the authoress of over two hundred
romantic novels.

As she lingered over her coffee and watched people
going up and down the steps of the Casino, Kathryn supposed she was lucky to have the sort of job which made
it possible for her to be living near this cosmopolitan
place, gilded Monte Carlo which for generations had
meant music and flowers, high fashion and expensive
jewellery, Mardi Gras and million-dollar yachts, diamonds and gambling, Grand Prix auto racing. . . .

Her thoughts screeched to a stop like a fast-travelling
car screeches to a halt when an obstacle rears up in its
way. Her oval-shaped, creamy-skinned face was smooth
and expressionless as she looked round and signalled to
the waiter who had served her. Only a slightly strained
look around her dark-lashed amber eyes and the nervous
movement of her delicately tinted soft lips betrayed that
inwardly she was disturbed by a sudden rush of
memories.

Memories of being in Monte with Cesare that first time
during Grand Prix week, dancing with him, laughing
with him, driving with him along the coast road to watch
the moonlight silver the sea, making love with him. . . .

The waiter brought her bill. She paid him and leaving
the café crossed the sunlit square again to the small blue
car parked below the casino steps. Unlocking the door,
she ducked inside and soon she was driving out of the
town.

The road to L'Hermitage was typical of Monaco. It
wound up a steep hillside in a series of hairpin bends,

sometimes hanging dizzily over the brilliant mocking sea, sometimes boring through a dark tunnel. Kathryn drove skilfully, concentrating all the time on what she was doing because to be careless on this road was to endanger one's life. There were several villas to pass, each one built on a bluff of rock above flower-hung terraced gardens, before she reached the dazzling white gateposts which guarded the drive to L'Hermitage.

The drive wound between green spear-like cypress trees and ended in front of an elegant white house which had been built at the beginning of the century to the orders of some Balkan prince who had spent most of his life in exile here. Constance Dale, that shrewd business woman, had bought it comparatively cheaply before the real estate boom in Monaco and the property was now reputed to be worth a million dollars.

Kathryn parked the car in the shade in a courtyard at the side of the house. Collecting parcels from the rear seat, she stepped out of the vehicle and slammed the door shut. At once she noticed the other car which was parked in the shade. It was long, low and white, and she recognised the make at once. It was the latest Vitelli sports, designed with jet-set playboys in mind, costing thousands of pounds.

About to step towards it to admire its powerful elegance more closely, Kathryn swung round abruptly, turning her back to it, and made her way quickly towards the side door of the house. Success and good management had brought Constance Dale a great deal of wealth and as a result the authoress had come into contact with other successful wealthy people who, taking advantage of Monaco's agreeable tax structure, had bought property there once belonging to the aristocrats of Europe where they spent the months of winter and drove about in cars like the Vitelli.

Vitelli, Vitelli—the name beat through Kathryn's head like the beat of the drums in the ceremony, almost like a warning as she entered the house and walked swiftly across the red-tiled floor of the central hall and into the long blue-walled, blue-carpeted lounge on her way to the terrace where she knew her employer would be having her lunch.

Daisy Hardcastle, one time school friend of Constance and now her housekeeper and cook, was coming across the lounge from one of the long french windows carrying a tray laden with dishes.

'Visitors?' Kathryn asked, her glance taking in the number of dishes on the tray.

'Aye, Mr Carey and another man. Didn't catch his name, foreigner of some sorts by the looks of him,' Daisy sniffed superciliously. 'Black hair and swarthy skin. Handsome, if you go for them Latin types—I don't. They came in that fancy car. Connie said to tell you she'd like to see you as soon as you came in.' Daisy went on towards the hall, then looked back from the archways. 'Did you get those stockings for me?'

'Yes. I hope they're the right colour. I'll leave the parcel here on this table.' Kathryn put the smallest parcel she was carrying on a highly polished oval side table and then dumped the other parcels on one of the ivory brocade armchairs. Going across to an elegant oval, gold-framed mirror which hung on the wall, she examined her appearance critically, smoothing a hand over the silkiness of her silvery hair. Once she had worn it loose in a tangle of waves and curls; now it was caught back severely into a chignon at the top of her head. The style made her look older, cool and efficient, which was how she wanted to look.

Satisfied that her tailored dress of leaf-green linen trimmed with white was also suitable for her position as Constance Dale's secretary, she stepped out on to the terrace and walked over to a table at which three people were sitting under a large striped umbrella.

'So you're back at last!' Constance Dale's voice, husky because she smoked too many cigarettes, was sharp and Kathryn gave her employer a quick, wary glance as she approached the table.

The novelist was dressed in a voluminous caftan made from flower-printed see-through voile which she wore over an underslip of turquoise silk, a style of dress which helped to conceal her ample figure. In the shade of the umbrella her ash-blonde wig glittered like silver foil and above the rouged pink of her fat cheeks her grey eyes also glittered coldly between thickly mascaraed lashes as she stared at her secretary.

'You remember John Carey?' she said. 'I think you met him when he was here last. He's been in Monte the past week for the Grand Prix auto races.'

Big and burly in a rather creased lightweight grey suit, John Carey, well-known popular painter who had made a fortune painting and selling warm vivid scenes of the Mediterranean fishing ports and holiday resorts, blundered to his feet politely.

'Hello, Mr Carey. It's nice to see you again,' said Kathryn.

'Nice to see you too.' He smiled at her warmly, but his shrewd blue eyes held a puzzled expression. He turned slowly towards the other younger man who had also risen to his feet. 'I don't think I have any need to introduce you to Luigi Vitelli. From all accounts you've known one another longer than I have known either of you.'

'*Come stà*, Kathryn,' said Luigi, his dark eyes glinting appreciatively as their glance swept over her. 'Long time no see.'

'*Bene, grazie—e lei?*' Kathryn answered automatically in Italian, speaking stiffly as she tried to hide the shock of surprise which ran through her like a cold shiver at the sight of him.

The same age as herself and about the same height that she was, he was wearing a vivid red open-necked shirt under a short-waisted battle-dress style jacket made from cream linen which matched his pants. Swarthy-skinned and black haired, with bold Roman features and glittering black eyes, he was the 'latin type' Daisy didn't care for.

'*Bene, grazie,*' he replied with a polite inclination of his head.

'What are you doing here?' Kathryn asked, again in Italian.

'Sit down, love,' ordered Constance curtly. 'You've never told me you could speak Italian.'

'I can speak a little, enough to get by,' replied Kathryn defensively as she pulled out the fourth and vacant chair and sat down. Immediately the two men resumed their seats.

'You didn't tell me either that you're married to Signor Vitelli's elder brother and that you're now separated from him,' Constance continued reproachfully.

Across the table Kathryn gave Luigi an irritated glance. Now she knew why Constance was angry. The novelist had found out that her secretary had deceived her.

'I had to tell Signora Dale why I wanted to see you and

why I know you as Kathryn Vitelli,' Luigi explained in slow careful English in answer to her unspoken question.

'Why do you want to see me?' she asked. 'Did Cesare send you?' It wouldn't be the first time Cesare had used his brother as a go-between, she thought bitterly, remembering the number of times Luigi had been sent to tell her that Cesare had been delayed and would be late returning from the Vitelli factory or from the racing circuit.

'No, he didn't.' He studied her with sombre eyes and for once his mobile mouth, usually so quick to smile, was set in a grim line. 'But it is on his account I am here to ask you. . . .'

'Wait a moment.' John Carey broke in as he pushed his chair back and rose to his feet. 'Constance, my dear, what Signor Vitelli has to tell Kathryn is hardly any of our business, so why don't you show me that painting you've been telling me about, the one you say is by Picasso?'

Constance frowned, glanced at Kathryn and then at Luigi.

'Kathryn, are you sure. . . .' she began, only to be interrupted by John, who had stepped behind her chair, with his hands resting on its back ready to pull it back when she stood up.

'Kathryn will explain everything to you later, I expect,' he said quietly.

'Oh, all right, then.' Constance stood up rather ungraciously. 'I know you think I've been hoaxed, but come and see it for yourself,' she muttered. Suddenly remembering her manners, she turned back to Luigi and smiled at him brilliantly. 'Excuse me,' she said. 'I'll see you before you go, of course, to give you that autographed copy of one of my books for your sister.'

'*Grazie, signorina*. You are most kind.' Luigi smiled too.

After glancing again at Kathryn Constance obeyed the pressure of John's hand on her elbow and with her multi-coloured caftan billowing about her like sails which have been puffed out by the wind, she went with him across the terrace towards the house.

Her eyes wide with incredulity, Kathryn watched Luigi sit down again.

'You have asked Constance to autograph a copy of one of her books for Cecilia?' she asked incredulously.

'*Si*, I have. It was the only excuse I could think of for coming to her house and seeing you.'

'How did you know I was here?'

'I saw you shopping in the Boulevard Princess Charlotte last Saturday.'

'Then why didn't you come and speak to me?'

'You moved away before I could. I saw you get into a car and drive away and since my car was parked nearby I was able to follow you to this house.'

'I didn't see you.'

'I intended that you shouldn't,' he retorted with his quick mischievous grin. 'By the time I reached the house you had gone inside.'

'You could have come to the door and asked for me.'

'I did. The housekeeper said that no Signora Vitelli lived here.' His mouth twisted wryly and his glance went to her ringless left hand with which she was fiddling with one of the empty wine glasses still left on the table. She put the glass down and folded her hands on her lap below the table edge where he couldn't see them.

'It is a beautiful house, this,' went on Luigi conversationally. 'And your employer seems to be a kindly person. You like the job, hmm?'

'Yes ... yes, I do.'

'It is better than being Cesare's wife, eh? You feel happy and independent?'

'Luigi, will you get to the point and tell me why you've wangled your way into this house. . . .'

'*Mi scusi*,' he interrupted, looking puzzled. 'What is this word—*wangled*? I do not know it. Translate into Italian, please.'

Kathryn gritted her teeth. It was no use getting angry with Luigi, she knew from past experience. Being of a naturally confident and optimistic disposition, he would never believe anyone could be angry with him and he shrugged off other people's anger like a duck shakes water from its back.

'It means that you lied and tricked your way into this house. You deceived Constance.'

'I do not think so. I was diplomatic,' he argued. 'And what was deceitful about asking for her autograph for Cecilia?'

'You know your sister doesn't read romantic novels. She has no more time for romance than ... than ... you have or Cesare has or any other members of your family have,' she accused.

'*Si*, that is true,' he agreed, nodding his head. 'We are not romantics. Being Italians we are realists. We prefer to experience everything through our senses rather than through our imaginations. For example,' he went on, warming to his argument, 'I prefer to drive a racing car in a Grand Prix event than to imagine I am driving a racing car. I prefer to make love to a woman I admire than to imagine I am making love to her. Cesare is the same.' He paused, gave her another sombre glance and added slowly, 'Or he was.'

Kathryn shifted uneasily in her chair and avoided his eyes. In the hot sunlit silence she could hear bees buzzing as they visited the pink and purple bell-like flowers of the creeper which tumbled over the stone balustrade of the terrace and far away, down the hill, came the groaning whine of a car's engine as the vehicle crawled up a steep gradient.

'Is Cesare in Monte?' she asked abruptly.

'No. He is in Italy.'

'Didn't he come for the Grand Prix, then? Didn't he race?' she exclaimed.

'*Non capisco*.' Luigi shook his head in puzzlement. 'I do not understand why you ask those questions. Cesare has not raced for over a year.'

'Not raced? Why?'

'Is it possible you do not know?' he demanded.

'Know what?'

'That he has not raced since he was hurt in an accident last year?'

Again Kathryn felt shock shiver through her, chilling her and causing her heart to miss a beat.

'No, I didn't know,' she whispered. 'No one told me.'

'But it was in the newspapers, on the radio and TV.'

'I didn't read about it, didn't hear about it,' she replied. She had avoided the parts of newspapers where reports of car racing events were printed, had deliberately cut herself off from that other world of excitement, noise and sudden violent death.

'But ... but ...' Luigi was now looking very troubled. 'Mamma wrote to tell you,' he said.

'At what address? Where did she send the letter?'

'To the address Tony gave us. You see, he had no idea where you had gone when you left Milan. Cesare never told us and there was nothing among his letters and papers. . . .'

'Tony?' she interrupted him. 'You mean Tony Baxter? He was there? At the accident?'

'*Si*. He was racing that day too. He told us his wife's parents might know where you were. He said her mother is your aunt and that you had lived with them after your mother died.'

'I didn't get the letter,' she mumbled between stiff lips. 'They couldn't send it on to me because they didn't know where I was either. But never mind that now. Tell me about Cesare. Was he badly hurt?'

'*Si*. The car caught fire and so did his overalls. His body was burned. His spinal cord was damaged and he was in a coma for many weeks.' Luigi looked very sad and heaved a sigh. 'We didn't expect him to live. Then we were afraid that if he did live he would have to be supported by machines. We prayed, all of us—*Dio mio*, how we prayed for him to die quickly, a swift release. Or if he survived to be as he once was, active and vigorous.' A smile lit the darkness of his eyes. 'Our prayers were answered. He came out of the coma. His burns healed and he learned to walk again. It was a miracle, a triumph over great odds. We rejoiced—and then we realised something was very wrong with him.'

'What was it?' whispered Kathryn, feeling her flesh creep.

'He had forgotten everything. He had lost his memory. He had forgotten who we were and who he was. He had forgotten he is the brilliant designer of car engines and a great racing driver.'

'Amnesia?' gasped Kathryn.

'That is right. The nerve specialists and the psychiatrists said it was due to the great shock he had suffered as a result of the accident. He was going very fast at the time. They said that given time his memory would return. We would just have to be very patient and do all we could to help him.' Luigi shook his head slowly from side to side. 'We have been very patient, we have done all we can for months now, hoping that he might say one day he had remembered something or someone.'

'Has he?'

'It is very difficult for us to tell. He has remembered how to drive and how to design, but he seems to have no memory of his life before the accident or of the accident itself and what caused it.'

'Then I suppose he doesn't remember being married to me,' she whispered.

'You are right. It seems that way.'

'Have you told him?'

'*Si*, we told him when we were trying to find out how much he did remember.'

'What did he say?'

'He laughed at us. Asked us to prove he had a wife by producing you. It was then that my mother wrote to you again. The letter was returned by your aunt with a note saying she had no idea where you were. Once again I met Tony at a race meeting and I asked him if he knew where you were, and he said he hadn't see you for over a year.' Luigi have her a searching look. 'Was he telling the truth, Kathryn?'

'Of course he was. I haven't seen him since the last

time I watched Cesare race.' Painful memory flooded
her mind suddenly. It was after that race, the day after
it, that she and Cesare had quarrelled. It was after that
quarrel that she had left him. 'Have you told him that I
left him?' she asked tentatively.

'Not yet. We, the whole family, have been hoping to
find you. We have been hoping that a meeting with you
might help him to remember more. The doctors now believe it is hysterical amnesia from which he is suffering.'

'What does that mean?'

'He is refusing to look back beyond a certain point in
his life.'

'The crash, in fact.'

'Si. They say that something unpleasant must have
happened to him just before the race, something he
doesn't want to remember and his mind is turning off as a
sort of protective mechanism.' He leaned forward with a
pleading expression in his eyes. 'I have found you at last,
Kathryn, and I am asking you to come back to Italy with
me, to see Cesare.'

'No, no ... I can't. I couldn't.' Her reaction was instinc-
tive, another protective mechanism going into action. 'I
have to stay here. Constance is in the middle of her next
book. I have to help her finish it.'

'But Kathryn....'

'Please don't ask me again,' she said hoarsely.

There was a strained silence as he stared at her and she
cringed inwardly when she saw contempt take the place
of surprise in his eyes.

'So, it is as I have suspected for some time,' he accused.
'You do not care for Cesare. You have never cared for
him, and that is why you did not come in answer to our
first letter to you.'

'I didn't receive it, honestly,' she protested.

'But even if you had you wouldn't have come, would you? Because you do not care,' he said between taut lips. 'You accuse me of lying, but you are guilty of the worst sort of lie. You lied when you married Cesare, when you promised to love and cherish him in sickness and in health.' His glance raked her. 'You're a cold unfeeling bitch and I can see now that Cesare is wise not to remember he is married to you.' He sprang to his feet. '*Mi scusi,*' he added. 'I must say goodbye to Signorina Dale and thank her for the autograph.'

'Luigi, wait!' Kathryn went after him and he turned to face her with his mouth curling in a contemptuous sneer.

'For what? For you to explain why you can't come with me? No, thank you. I would rather not hear any more of your weak excuses,' he jeered.

'Please, just tell me one thing. Where is Cesare living?' she asked.

'Why do you want to know?'

'I'll write to him. If he receives a letter from me it will prove to him that I exist and that we're ... we're still married, won't it?'

'What would you put in the letter?' he demanded suspiciously.

'I would tell him we were married three years ago and why ... why I'm not living with him. It could do what you want. It could help him remember without him and me having to meet.'

He frowned at her in puzzlement.

'You're afraid of seeing him, again, aren't you?' he scoffed. 'You're afraid of confrontation.'

'I ... er ... no, I'm not.'

'Then come with me,' he pleaded again. 'Come and see him.'

'Please tell me where he's living so I can send a letter,' she said woodenly.

'No, but I'll do something else. If you write the letter I'll take it to him for you. Considering how letters from us to you have failed to reach you perhaps it would be safer for me to take it. I'm staying another night at Loews Hotel. You can let me know when you have written it and I'll come out here to collect it.' He paused and gave her another contemptuous glance. 'But if you care, Kathryn, if you really care, you won't just write to him. You'll come with me to-morrow.'

'I'll write the letter, I promise, and you can take it,' she said, ignoring his pleading, and turning on her heel she went across the terrace quickly, half-running as if to escape from something which threatened her.

In the comfortable study-lounge where she worked every day and sometimes in the evenings she went straight to the wide desk and sat down behind it. Opening a drawer, she took out a folder and placed it on top of the desk. She took her reading glasses from her handbag and slipped them on, picked up a ballpoint pen, opened the folder and began to read the top pages of a thick sheaf of typewritten quarto-sized paper.

Work was the best antidote to worry about her relationship to Cesare, she had discovered over the past eighteen months, ever since she had left him. Work until her eyes were aching and she was ready to drop with fatigue. Work until her mind was numb and she was incapable of indulging in regret for what had been and for something which was even more painful, what might have been.

She read quickly, pen in hand, ready to correct misspelled words or to add a left-out question mark or full-stop, all the time on the alert for other mistakes. Constance Dale's novels were popular not only for their simple romantic stories set in historical periods such as Regency England or Tzarist Russia or Louis the Fourteenth's France but also for the easy-to-read style in which they were written, a style Constance had perfected over the years with the help of the secretaries she had employed to type her work and correct it.

Kathryn had turned over several pages before she realised she hadn't made one correction, hadn't in fact been reading properly at all but had been merely skimming the typewritten words with her eyes not taking in their sense at all because her thoughts were not engaged in what she was doing.

Damn! She tossed the ballpoint pen down and whipping off her glasses rubbed her fingers across her eyes. She couldn't concentrate, and she knew why. Cesare was on her mind. Cesare whom she had tried so hard to forget. After a year and a half she thought she had become immune to him. She had even thought she could have met him face to face without feeling any emotion at all. But here she was, shot all to pieces because Luigi had turned up unexpectedly and had asked her to go to Italy to see Cesare and she had refused.

Why had she refused? Luigi's contemptuous accusations as to why she had rang in her ears and she groaned. He had been right, she was afraid to see Cesare again; afraid the sight of him might churn up emotions in her she would rather not feel; afraid she might find Sophia living with him.

Yet it was Luigi's suggestion that she had lied when she

had married Cesare which had hurt most, because it was true. She hadn't married Cesare because she had loved him. Love hadn't been part of that brief one-day courtship which had led to them eloping to be married in a hasty civil ceremony over the border in France. Passion, yes, surging through both of them, a wild spring tide under the influence of the full moon, but not love. She had married Cesare in a gesture of defiance, to show Tony Baxter and her cousin Jane Hart that she didn't care. . . .

Elbows on the desk, cheeks between her hands, Kathryn stared at the window, not seeing the pale waxy blooms of the magnolia tree etched against a clear blue sky outside. For she was seeing again her cousin's face glowing with happiness, hearing again Tony's voice shouting above the noise of disco music announcing that he and Jane had become engaged to be married; Tony whom she had loved for so long, ever since she had turned seventeen, and who she had hoped would one day ask her to marry him.

She had been unable to bear the sight of Jane's face any longer, nor had she been able to sit there and join in the noisy congratulations which had been offered to the couple. She had sprung to her feet, had turned away from the table in the night-club where they had been celebrating the end of the Grand Prix week and had dodged between the swaying dancers, not sure where she had been going but determined to escape.

Out of the whirling, light-flickering semi-darkness a hand had grasped her arm and a masculine voice had shouted in her ear:

'Come and dance with me.'

She had recognised him, of course, even though they

hadn't been formally introduced. Handsome, successful,
self-confident, Cesare Vitelli had been the dynamic leader
of the Vitelli racing team, with a reputation for having
a way with women. He had been smiling down at her,
assuming no doubt that she would give in at once and
dance with him.

'No,' she had retorted, and had tried to pull free.

'Yes,' he had hissed, and with one tug on her arm
swung her into his arms. 'It doesn't do to say no to me,'
he had whispered into the thickness of her hair. 'Refusal
only makes me more determined to have my own way,
and tonight is special. Tonight I'm king of the castle. I'm
the winner, and winner takes all. . . .'

At that moment Kathryn had noticed Jane and Tony
walk on to the dance floor, melting into each other's arms
as the music had changed to something slow, sweet and
sentimental, and suddenly she hadn't wanted to be alone
any more. She had wanted company, cheerful, lively
company. She had wanted to be held closely too, and to
dance, if not with Tony then with some other man, because it was possible that in close contact she might find
forgetfulness. Recklessly she had put her arms about
Cesare's neck and tipping back her head had looked up
into the dark enigmatic depths of his eyes.

'All right, king of the castle,' she had said, smiling at
him, 'I'll dance with you.'

He had been in high spirits as a result of the many
successes he had had on the racing circuit that week. As
he had boasted, he was the winner, and as a result was in
the running for the world championship, a goal for which
he had been aiming ever since he had started to race
cars as a youth.

His elation had woven a spell about Kathryn, trapping

her at his side for the rest of the night so that when Jane had approached her to tell her she and Tony and the rest of the people from Britain who were with them were leaving to go back to the hotel she had refused.

'But you can't stay here on your own,' Jane had whispered.

'I'm not on my own. I'm with Cesare,' Kathryn had replied defiantly. 'And I'm staying with him.'

At that moment Cesare had been involved in a noisy, laughing conversation with members of the Italian racing team who were also celebrating his success in the races. Jane had given him a sidelong critical glance and had turned back to Kathryn.

'You can't stay with him, Kathryn. You don't know what he's like,' she had remonstrated. 'His reputation with women stinks.'

'So what?' Kathryn had retorted. 'Think I can't take care of myself?'

'I think you're in a very strange mood,' Jane had countered sharply. 'What have you been drinking?'

'Nothing. I don't have to drink to enjoy myself. Go on, Jane, go back to the hotel with Tony. I'm going to dance all night. See you to-morrow.'

She and Cesare had danced all night—well, nearly all night. It had been close on three o'clock in the morning when they had finally left the night-club. Outside the night air had been mild, the sky dark blue, sprinkled with a myriad stars and lit by moonglow.

'Let's go and look at the moonlight on the sea,' Cesare had suggested, and taking her hand had led her through the narrow streets to the big hotel, seven graceful tiers of rooms angled above the sea where he was staying and where his car was parked.

Soon the elegant powerful Vitelli car had been roaring along the twisting coast road. Kathryn had never found out exactly where they had stopped along that road, but the view over the sea that night had been fantastically romantic with the rays of the full moon flecking the water with silvery light. The only sounds had been the quiet *shush* of waves on rocks, the perpetual chirp of crickets on the cliffs behind and the sudden swift beat of her heart when Cesare had put his arm about her shoulders and had drawn her against him.

Against the bareness of her throat his lips had been warm and at their touch little flames had seemed to flicker tantalisingly along her nerves. He had whispered something in Italian which she hadn't understood.

'What did you say?' she had asked, and had moved away from him slightly so that she could see his face. Silvered by moonlight, the bold strong features had looked as if they had been carved from precious metal.

'The usual English translation is—"Lovely maid in the moonlight". It's a quotation from an Italian opera,' he had replied in English, his accent giving the language a fascinatingly attractive lilt.

'I know. It's from *La Bohème*.' She had felt suddenly and strangely breathless as he had shifted along the seat to be near her again.

'And it describes you, right now,' he had whispered, and raising a hand had trailed a lazy fingertip down her cheek, down her throat right down to the cleft between her breasts, revealed by the low cut of her evening dress.

'You're making fun of me again,' she had protested, her breath catching in her throat. She had already learned that he had a lively satirical sense of humour. She had pushed his hand away, but with a deft movement he had turned it and had trapped her fingers in it. Raising them to his lips, he had kissed each one of them in turn.

'I do not make fun now,' he had countered softly, leaning closer so that she had felt the warmth of his breath in her cheek. 'I make love. And you are lovely. Your skin as soft as silk, your hair spun from sunbeams, your eyes bright as stars, your lips ... ah, there is only one way to praise your lips, pretty maid.' And bending his head, he had kissed them.

She had been in no condition to resist the warm temptation of that kiss and her lips had moved against his in response. Her arms had gone round his neck and her fingers had wound in the thick close-cropped curls of his black hair.

His mouth had opened over hers demandingly, forcing hers to open too, and his hand had slid up to cup one of her breasts. Her mind had reeled and for the first time in her life she had savoured the hot sweet taste of physical desire.

Oblivious to everything but the sensuous feel of his mouth on hers and the tender torture of his finger-tips stroking her skin, she had given in completely to the exciting sensations which had swept through her body. Pressing against him, caressing him where she could with inexpert fingers, she had found that being close to him, being intimate with him, had brought the ease she had hoped it would. She had stopped thinking and hurting and for the next hour Tony and Jane had been forgotten completely as Cesare had been her guide in the exploration of the pleasures of passion.

Later, still in his arms, she had watched the darkness fade from the sky, as the pearly fingers of dawn pushed it away, and the sea change slowly from dark blue to pale violet grey.

'Where do you go when you leave Monte?' Cesare had asked casually.

'Back to England.' With the words she had come down to earth and cold, cold reality, remembering Jane and Tony were engaged. How could she go back with them and pretend it didn't matter? she had thought miserably. How could she go to their wedding and not show she was heartbroken? How could she go on with life? She had shivered suddenly.

'You are cold?' Cesare's hand had been warm on her bare arm and he had held her closer.

'Not when you hold me like this,' she had muttered into his shoulder. 'I ... I ... don't want to go back to England,' she had added.

'Then don't go back. Stay with me.' His lips had moved gently against the tender skin of her temple. 'Stay and live with me.' Then he had added, his voice deeply persuasive, 'Sleep with me.'

'I don't see how I can,' she had mumbled, but her heart had leapt up and had begun to beat wildly.

'Do you have to go back? Do you have parents or family who are expecting your return?'

'No. I don't have any parents. My father raced cars too and he was killed in an accident when I was a baby, and my mother died six years ago.'

'*Mi dispiace*—I'm sorry.' His voice had been quiet and sympathetic 'So you don't have to ask anyone's permission?'

'Permission to do what?'

'To marry me.'

For a moment she had been perfectly still, frozen in

position by surprise. Then she had raised her head from his shoulder to look at him. In the pale early morning light his face had been different, the chin blurred by black beard stubble, the cheeks hollow, the eyelids drooping lazily from lack of sleep, but it had been no more revealing than it had been by moonlight and his eyes, which she had realised for the first time were not black but a dark obsidian green, had been empty of expression as they had met hers.

'When? Where?' she had asked incredulously.

'As soon as we can, wherever we can,' he had replied.

'You ... you ... mean it?'

'I mean it.' His well shaped lips had quivered slightly in amusement. 'Do you have to ask permission?'

'No, no, oh no. I ... I'm over eighteen. I'm twenty-one. I can make my own decisions.'

'For that I am glad,' he had murmured with another quiver of amusement, then had added more seriously, 'Will you marry me, Katryn, *per favore?*'

The way he had said her name, his inability to pronounce the 'th' in the English way had somehow made him even more endearing.

'Yes, yes, please,' she had replied recklessly, and overcome suddenly by shyness, behaving as if he had never kissed her or touched her, she had buried her face against his neck.

'*Grazie,*' he had said with a touch of dryness, and without saying any more he had started the engine of the car. Still with one arm about her, holding her close against him, he had driven back towards the hill-climbing terraces of Monte Carlo's glittering space-saving buildings.

In fifteen minutes they had been in the lift in the hotel

where Kathryn had been staying on the way to her room. He had helped her pack her cases and had even told her what to put in the note she had left for Jane to find. Then they had driven to the other hotel where he had collected his luggage and had checked out. By seven-thirty they had been on their way to the French border again. By nightfall that day they had been married.

CHAPTER TWO

THE sound of voices, the slamming of a car's doors, the familiar muffled roar of a powerful engine starting up brought Kathryn out of her reverie. Slipping on her glasses again, she bent over the typescript and made another conscious effort to concentrate. She succeeded and for the next hour passed quickly as she read and corrected. So absorbed was she in what she was doing that she didn't look up when the door of the study opened and Constance swept in.

'How is it going?' asked the novelist as she crossed the room like a ship in full sail.

'Fine,' replied Kathryn shortly. 'I've nearly finished correcting all that I've typed up so far.'

'Good.' Constance helped herself to a cigarette from a box on the desk, fitted it into a long jade holder, lit it with the heavy solid silver table lighter which had been a gift from an admirer of hers and moved in the direction of the chaise-longue from which most of her novels had been dictated over the past few years. Sitting down, she swung her legs up and leaned back against plump silk-covered cushions. She arranged her caftan becomingly, inhaled several times from her cigarette, then said,

'Another chapter should finish it, don't you think? Where did we leave Melissa and Rudolpho?'

'Travelling across the Russian steppes wrapped in furs on a horse-drawn sleigh,' said Kathryn coolly, opening another drawer in the desk and taking out a thick stenographer's notebook. Pencil poised, she waited for Constance to start dictating.

When nothing happened she looked up. Constance was staring at her through the haze of smoke, her grey eyes narrowed thoughtfully. Looking down at the blank page of the notebook Kathryn made a fantastic doodle on the top of it and held her hand in front of her mouth to stifle a yawn. The afternoon was warm and sleep-provoking. She would have liked to have been sunbathing beside a swimming pool.

'Why didn't you tell me you're married to Cesare Vitelli?' Constance spoke sharply and Kathryn jumped, not being prepared for such an abrupt question.

'I didn't think it was necessary to tell you,' she replied calmly, continuing to doodle on the pad and giving, she hoped, an appearance of indifference to the question.

'Not necessary?' exclaimed Constance. Kathryn glanced at her warily. The novelist had sat up and was stubbing out the end of her cigarette in an ash-tray on the occasional table beside the chaise-longue.

'I didn't think my marital status was any of your concern. I needed a job and you needed a good stenographer, a purely business relationship. Other more personal relationships either of us might have didn't enter into the arrangement,' said Kathryn, still doodling.

'By God, you're cool, I'll give you that,' said Constance tautly. 'But you're mistaken. Your marital status is and was my concern.'

'I don't see why,' retorted Kathryn.

'Didn't the secretarial agency which sent you to be interviewed tell you that I've never employed married women?'

'No. Why don't you?'

'For obvious reasons,' Constance snapped. 'A married

woman would want to be with her husband and children, quite rightly so too. I have never employed a woman who has been married and divorced or separated either.'

'You employ Daisy, and she's been married,' Kathryn pointed out.

'Daisy is a widow, an entirely different situation,' hissed Constance angrily.

'I can't see why you shouldn't employ a woman who is divorced or separated from her husband. She's just as free as a single woman or a widow is.'

'That isn't the point,' retorted Constance. 'I have to consider my image as the queen of romantic fiction, and there's nothing romantic about divorce or separation. Now will you answer my question. Did the agency tell you that I never employed married women nor women who have been divorced or separated?' she rapped.

'No, but then I expect it was because it was believed I wasn't married. And when you interviewed me you didn't ask me.'

'So you deceived me deliberately by not using your married name. . . .'

'Many women who are married continue to be known at their work by their own last names,' Kathryn argued.

'And you didn't wear a wedding ring,' Constance accused, swinging off the chaise-longue and coming across to the desk to take another cigarette. Her eyes bright with anger, her rouged face a little haggard, she glared down at Kathryn. 'You didn't wear it and you don't wear it now, to deceive me,' she said in a taut whisper.

'I didn't wear it and I don't wear one because I don't have one,' replied Kathryn, her voice unsteady as she looked down at her ringless hands.

When they had been married in that secret hurried

civil ceremony in Nice, Cesare had taken the gold signet
ring which he had worn on the little finger of his right
hand and had pushed it on to the middle finger of her left
hand because it had been too big for the third finger. He
had promised to buy her a wedding ring as soon as possible. But he hadn't bought one and she had continued to
wear the signet ring because she had liked the engraving
of the phoenix rising from the ashes, which was the
Vitelli seal, for it had somehow expressed the growth of
her love for Cesare rising out of the ashes of her adoles-
cent crush on Tony. She had worn it until the day she
had left him. Then she had taken it off and had left it
with a note in an envelope to be given to him by the
reception clerk at the hotel where she had been staying
with Cesare at the time.

'You don't have one? Why not?' Again Constance
spoke sharply from the chaise-longue to which she had
returned, taking the box of cigarettes with her.

'Cesare didn't give me one,' Kathryn replied. 'Are you
going to dictate this afternoon, or can I get on with the
correction of this typescript?' she went on in a brisk busi-
nesslike tone. 'We're behind schedule, you know, and
we'll have to rush that last chapter if you're going to
meet your deadline.'

'Too many visitors. Too many interruptions, that's the
trouble,' Constance complained. 'And I can't dictate
while I have this problem of you on my mind. Knowing
you've been married and have separated has upset me,
quite disturbed the flow of romantic thought.' She glared
at Kathryn again through the smoke haze. 'What sort of a
man doesn't buy a wedding ring when he gets married?
Tell me that?' she demanded.

'A man who marries in a hurry.'

'Humph. Well, that's a romantic reason enough, I suppose,' Constance conceded reluctantly. 'John told me a little about this Cesare while we were looking at the painting. Seems John has been a fan of his over the years. He said he's quite brilliant both as a driver and a designer, the most brilliant star in a family of stars, apparently. Where did you meet him?'

'Here in Monte, three years ago, during Grand Prix week.'

'You've been here before?' Constance squeaked incredulously, then swallowed a mouthful of smoke accidentally and coughed wheezily for a few seconds. 'I'm disappointed in you, Kathryn,' she gasped.

'I'm sorry.'

'I believed you were like all the other stenographers I've employed over the years, young and fresh, virginal and innocent, truly romantic, waiting for Mr Right to come along and propose to you.' The grey glance raked Kathryn's face. 'God knows you look innocent enough with your smooth face and your big clear eyes, and you've certainly deceived me. I'd never have guessed you'd been in Monte before we came here.'

'I'd only been here for a week,' Kathryn defended herself.

'How did you get mixed up with the car racing set?'

'My uncle, my father's brother, is Rex Hart, chief designer for a British group which manufactures sport cars and racing cars. That year his daughter Jane and I came to Monte with him and his wife to watch the races. I met Cesare and ... and ... eloped with him.'

'Eloped? Good God, you can't be serious!'

'I am.'

'But why elope? Surely in this day and age no one

wanted to stop you from getting married.'

'I don't know whether anyone would have tried to stop us. We didn't tell anyone at the time. We ... I ... he ... both of us just wanted to get married quickly and quietly.'

'Because you were very much in love with each other?' suggested Constance hopefully, her eyes and her voice softening as she sensed romance.

'We were attracted to each other,' admitted Kathryn. 'But I don't think we were in love with each other in the way your characters are in love before they get married. It was only a physical attraction.'

'Meaning your hearts weren't involved, I suppose. Then you should never have married,' chided Constance severely. 'That's the message I'm always trying to convey. Physical attraction just isn't enough for marriage. Why did you leave him?'

'I found out he loved another woman,' muttered Kathryn, looking down at the pen she was twisting between her fingers. 'I thought that if I left him it might make it easier for him to divorce me so he could marry her.'

'I see,' Constance sighed. 'And has it made it easier for him? Is he going to divorce you? Is that why his brother wanted to see you, to tell you that?'

'No. Luigi came to tell me that Cesare is suffering from amnesia as a result of an accident he was in last year. The Vitelli family would like me to go and see him in the hope that a meeting with me might help him to remember more about his past life.'

'Mmm. Typically Italian. Everything must be done to restore their star to his former glory,' commented Constance, and gave Kathryn a sharp look. 'I don't suppose the family approve of you one little bit for walking out on him. And they won't be keen on divorce either. It would blemish the family name. Are you going to see him?'

'I told Luigi I couldn't go with him.'

'Couldn't?' Constance's glance was sharply suspicious. 'I hope you didn't say you couldn't go because of your job here. Oh, I can see that you did. I won't have it. I won't have you using me as an excuse.'

'But I can't leave you when you're nearly at the end of a story, and you're so behind schedule.'

'Listen to me, Kathryn.' Constance was suddenly very stern. 'I know I have a right to demand your loyalty as your employer and this is partly one of the reasons why I prefer to employ women who have no other attachments. But in this instance I'm quite willing to give you leave to go and see this man. He's still your husband and your loyalty should be to him first.'

'I don't see it that way,' argued Kathryn desperately. 'He wouldn't put me first just because I'm his wife.'

'How do you know? Have you tested him?'

'Yes, oh yes, many times. Always the racing the cars came first with him. I was way down on the list of his priorities,' Kathryn said bitterly. 'Anyway, I don't think I could bear it if his memory came back while I was with him and he remembered how much. . . .' She couldn't go on because suddenly her lips were trembling. The shock of hearing about Cesare, of learning that he had almost died, was catching up on her and her hard-won poise of cool indifference was fast breaking up.

'How much what, love? Come on, you can tell me. You've got to get it out of your system somehow. What are you afraid of him remembering?'

'How much he hates me,' Kathryn said huskily.

'He hated you?' exclaimed Constance. 'Why?'

'Because he had married me and was tied to me.'

Constance stared at her in puzzlement for a moment, then stubbed out her second cigarette.

'You're quite sure that what he felt for this other woman you mention wasn't just a passing thing, with him?' she asked eventually.

'Quite sure.'

'Was she married too?'

'She had been.'

'Divorced?'

'Widowed. Cesare had know her for years. They'd been almost engaged, once.'

'Almost? What happened.'

'Her parents didn't approve of him. They wanted her to marry a man of their choice.'

'A marriage of convenience between two important business families, I suppose,' said Constance dryly.

'Yes, Of course, she did what she was told. Her husband was sent to the United States to represent his company there and she went too. But he became ill and they had to return to Italy. Cesare and I had been married a little more than a year when he met her again. She'd come to watch him race. By then it was known her husband was dying.' Kathryn broke off and swallowed to steady her voice. 'I saw them meet. If you could have seen the way they looked at each other, the way they embraced, you'd have known it wasn't over between them. And after that Cesare was ... well, he treated me differently.'

'And you treated him differently too, I expect.' Again Constance was very dry, and Kathryn stiffened.

'I suppose I did,' she admitted.

'Showed you were jealous, nagged at him, denied him his conjugal rights, behaved in fact like a frightened bitch.'

'I wasn't frightened,' Kathryn retorted hotly. 'I was trying to make him be honest with me, to make him admit it wasn't me he wanted but her.'

'And did he?'

'Not in as many words, but he ... he told me to leave him, so I did.' Kathryn picked up her glasses and slid them on again. 'If you don't mind I'd rather not talk about it any more.'

Constance didn't reply but swung off the chaise-longue again and approached the desk. She helped herself to another cigarette and stood tapping the end of it on a fingernail, obviously deep in thought. Kathryn picked up her pen and tried to read the typescript, but once again her eyes only skimmed the page. She couldn't concentrate. Her thoughts were chaotic and her head was aching.

'Tell me about this amnesia he's suffering from,' said Constance. 'Has he forgotten everything? Oh, I know,' she added quickly as Kathryn gave her an exasperated glance, 'you don't want to talk about him. Because it hurts you, doesn't it? You can't *bear it*. Isn't that how you put it? My God, I'd have thought you'd have had more guts, more stamina.'

'I had the guts to leave him, didn't I?' Kathryn flared. 'Oh, what you know about it? You've never been married, never been subjected to the pressures of the relationship. . . .'

'How do you know I've never been married?' Constance interrupted her coldly, and Kathryn blinked in amazement.

'You don't wear any rings either,' she pointed out.

'Not on my left hand, no. I wear them on my right hand because they fit better there.' Constance held out her right hand. On the third finger below the blaze of a simple single diamond engagement ring a thin wedding ring glinted.

'I hadn't noticed,' murmured Kathryn.

'We were very happy, Morris and I, for several years,' Constance went on musingly. 'We met during the second world war. He was a soldier, I was a nurse. He was very badly wounded and I nursed him. Later, when the war was over, he died as a result of those wounds. So you see I do happen to know a little about those pressures you talk of. I know how complicated and close a relationship marriage is.' Constance's raking glance was as contemptuous as Luigi's had been. 'I also know how to love,' she added quietly. 'You don't.'

'I do, I do,' Kathryn protested huskily. 'I left him because I loved him—I loved him too much to stand in the way of his happiness.'

'What a lot of rot,' said Constance scornfully. 'And you're the one who believes in being honest and frank? You didn't leave him because you loved him. You left him because you couldn't cope with competition.'

'Why should I cope with it? Why should I put up with it?' Kathryn demanded hotly. 'Why should any woman put up with it?'

'That's better. That's more honest,' Constance commended. 'But I can't approve of your way of dealing with the situation. Running away never solved anything. Now tell me, has he forgotten everything?'

Kathryn told her in terse stilted sentences what Luigi had said about the state of Cesare's memory.

'Chances are, then, that he'd forgotten he ever had an

association with this other woman you talk about,' suggested Constance, perching on the edge of the desk. 'Had you thought of that?'

'No, I hadn't. But I don't think she would let him forget her. She would be there on the spot, you see, when he was hurt. She would visit him and possibly be invited by the family to go and see him to help him remember. Luigi said they've done everything they can think of to help Cesare.'

'And now they've invited you and you love him so little that you've refused to go and see him,' said Constance sternly. 'You don't love him, do you?'

'I ... I ... don't know. I can't be sure whether I do or not. I'd have to see him again....' Kathryn broke off as she realised what she had said.

'You know, I think I'm beginning to understand why Cesare asked you to leave him. Living with you must have been like being on a see-saw, very disconcerting. He wouldn't be able to depend on you, would he? It must have been like living with a child, a jealous, petty child. No wonder he turned to another woman!' remarked Constance cuttingly, and sailed away in the direction of the chaise-longue to plonk herself down on it again.

Biting her lip hard to check back another retort, Kathryn bent over the typescript again. The printed words blurred before her eyes.

'Are you going to fire me, because I'm married?' she managed to say at last.

'I'm glad you've asked that question,' said Constance, 'because I've been considering what to do. No, I'm not going to fire you, but I'm hoping you'll leave without notice to go and see your husband. I'm hoping you'll find the guts and the grace to go and see him at this time when he needs all the help he can get. I hope you have it in you to let bygones be bygones. And if you don't——' Constance paused impressively and Kathryn looked up enquiringly. 'If you decide not to go,' Constance went on serenely, 'then I will fire you on the grounds that you're not trustworthy or reliable. And now, if you're ready, I'd like to get on with that last chapter.'

It was after midnight when Kathryn went to bed that night, but the story of Melissa and Rudolpho was finished, brought to its romantic climax and happy ending. All that needed to be done was the final correction of the type-script before the story was put in an envelope and mailed to Constance Dale's publisher in London. That could be done in the morning, Kathryn decided, as she lay down and switched off the bedside lamp. Right now she was too tired, as she had hoped she would be. Too tired to do anything but sleep.

An hour later she was still awake, her head throbbing with pain and her thoughts full of Cesare. Turning on to her back, she stared up into the darkness. Did his head ache, she wondered, when he lay in bed? Did he toss and turn trying to remember?

Probably not. Hadn't Luigi said that Cesare didn't want to remember past a certain point in his life, past the point when he had crashed? Why had he crashed? She should have asked Luigi for more details. Now she was tormented by the usual questions. When? Where? How? And there was no way of finding the answers to the questions unless she went with Luigi to Italy in the morning.

It would have been Cesare's first serious accident since he had taken up racing. It had always been his boast that in all the years he had been racing he had never taken any unnecessary risks which might endanger the lives of other drivers, or of spectators or his own life. Had it been his fault or had another driver been involved? Or had something been wrong with the car? Brake failure or a punctured tyre? Oh, God, would she ever know? Why hadn't she asked Luigi?

Cesare was in a coma for months, Luigi had said. How she wished she had known! She would have gone to Cesare if she had known. She would have gone to sit by his bedside, praying and hoping with the rest of the Vitelli family, with his parents, his two sisters and two brothers, praying he might have a quick release or survive to be as he had been.

For Cesare to be a vegetable supported by life-giving machines would have hurt terribly anyone who had known him and loved him. He wouldn't have wanted it either. He would have preferred to die swiftly, for his life to be clicked off like a light is clicked off.

But now, after all, he was a cripple, in a way; his mind was crippled by amnesia. Kathryn turned restlessly, tormented by a new thought. If Luigi had told her that Cesare was crippled physically and couldn't walk, what would she have done? Would she have gone to him to look after him as a wife was expected to do?

You don't care. You have never cared, Luigi had said. *You don't love him, do you?* Constance had accused. Kathryn groaned as she examined her feeling. She did care, she cared desperately. She wouldn't be lying here awake, would she, if she didn't care?

It was true she hadn't married Cesare because she had loved him, but she had learned to love him during the time she had lived with him, had loved him more than anyone else she had known. That was why she had been so upset when Sophia had come back into his life, and swamped suddenly by new violent emotions, totally incapable of dealing with them, she had attacked him, lashing out at him verbally and so giving him cause to hate her.

She had acted childishly and he had told her to leave and that should have been the end. As far as she was concerned it had been the actual end of their marriage if not the legal end. So why should she be expected to go and see him now? And what good would it do him seeing her again? If he didn't want to remember wasn't he better off that way? Remembering the crash and what had gone before might only bring him more suffering.

Groaning again, Kathryn tossed about in the bed. If only she could stop thinking about him, wondering how he looked whether he was any different. She would like to see him again. The thought sidled into her mind from nowhere, making her suddenly still. Wide-eyed, she watched the dawn fill the bedroom with grey light. She must see him again to find out if she still loved him; to find out why he had crashed; to find out why he hadn't answered the one letter she had written to him; to find out why he hadn't done anything about divorcing her. It was the only way.

Her head aching, her eyes sore from sleeplessness, she slid from the bed and went to the window to watch the distant sea change from violet-grey to rose-tinted blue as the sun came up, remembering with a vividness which made her catch her breath the morning she and Cesare had watched the sun rise when he had asked her to marry him. The night of torment over, she felt strangely calm, and as she stood there remembering his gentleness that day three years ago she knew suddenly what she was going to do.

In the bathroom she showered and shampooed her hair. After blow-drying her hair she pinned it up into its customary topknot, then dressed in a lightweight knife-pleated skirt and loose-fitting silky blouse. She looked very pale after the bad night and there were black smudges under her amber eyes, so she applied make-up rather heavily to hide the ravages. Then she went downstairs to have breakfast as usual with Daisy in the kitchen. When she had finished her meal she went to the study and took her place behind the desk. She took out the typescript of Constance's story and put it on the top of the desk.

It would be better to phone Luigi before she started work, she decided, and pulled the telephone towards her. In a few minutes the phone was ringing in his room. She had to let it ring several times before he answered. His voice was gruff and sleepy, but cleared when he recognised who it was phoning him.

'Ah, Kathryn, *buon giorno. Come stà?* Have you written your letter to Cesare yet? Do you want me to come and pick it up?' he asked cheerfully.

'No, I haven't written a letter. Luigi . . . I've decided to come with you and see him.'

'You have? But this is wonderful! I am so glad. . . .' He broke off and she heard him muttering rapidly in Italian to someone who was obviously with him in the room.

'Luigi, who are you talking to?' she asked.

'Tina, my wife,' he replied.

'You're married?' she exclaimed.

'But of course. What is so strange about that? And next month, God willing, I become a father.' He chuckled. 'I beat Cesare to it after all, hmm? Tina says she is looking forward to meeting you. When shall I come for you? Ten o'clock? Ten-thirty?'

'About eleven. Or is that too late?'

'No, no, of course not. Any time you say.'

'I have some work to finish before I leave.'

'So that is all arranged,' he said. 'I go now. I must phone Mamma to tell her to expect you this evening. See you later, Kathryn.'

Now she was committed she felt much better and was able to concentrate better on the work she had to do. At the end of an hour and a half she had finished correcting the story. She clipped each chapter together with a paper clip and slipping the whole typescript into a folder she went up to Constance's bedroom, tapped on the door and entered.

The novelist was sitting up in bed, sipping orange juice and leafing through a newspaper. Over the top of her reading spectacles she peered at Kathryn.

'Hello, you're early,' she remarked. 'Aren't you touring Monte this morning?'

'No, I decided to finish this.' Kathryn went forward and laid the folder on the bedside table. 'I thought you might want to look through it before it's mailed.'

'Mmm, I should, I suppose,' murmured Constance, leaning back against her pillows. 'You look as if you had a rough night of it. Come to any decision?'

'Yes. I'm going to see Cesare. Luigi is coming for me in half an hour. I'm going to pack now.'

'Good for you! I had a feeling you'd see sense. You can't run away from reality for ever, you know. You have to grow up some time and take on the responsibility for your own actions. Trite but true. Go and see him, meet him face to face and see what happens. If he remembers then take it from there, talk it out.'

'I'll try,' whispered Kathryn.

'And if he doesn't remember ... well, the whole situation will have the most exciting and romantic possibilities.'

'In what way?'

'You could fall in love with each other,' suggested Constance with a twinkle in her eyes.

'Doesn't that romantic imagination of yours ever rest?' teased Kathryn.

'Not if I can help it. But to be serious, Kathryn. Leave anything you don't need immediately here. I'll send it on to you if necessary. You'll let me know how things go, won't you?'

'Copy for your next novel?' mocked Kathryn.

'No, because I'll be anxious about you. And remember if it doesn't work out I'll be glad to have you back. Married or unmarried, you're a damned good stenographer and secretary. Best I've ever had.'

CHAPTER THREE

THE bus from Milan swept through yet another tunnel bored through the hard rock of the Italian Alps and out once again into the mellow sunlight of late afternoon. From the window beside which she was sitting Kathryn had a clear view of Lake Minore, the smallest of the gem-like lakes which glitter among the purple and sometimes snow-covered slopes of the lofty mountains. Close to the edge of the lake the clustered roofs of the village of Molino bloomed like geranium flowers, glowing red against the sapphire blue background of the smooth water of the lake.

Kathryn felt the nerves in her stomach flutter and tighten with apprehensive excitement. She was almost at the end of her journey. In a few minutes she would step off the bus into the village square and would meet Cesare again. She was very sure she would recognise him immediately. But would he recognise her? Would memory return to him in a flash when he saw her as his family were hoping it would?

It had been Cesare's mother, the dark-haired, swarthy-skinned, Roman-nosed Emilia Vitelli, that energetic devoted Italian mother, who managed her husband and her children in a subtle, imperceptible way, who had suggested almost casually that Kathryn should go alone to the Vitellis' lakeside villa to see Cesare.

'If Kathryn is by herself and if he doesn't know she is coming there will be more surprise, more shock and perhaps more chance that he will remember,' she had said as she had served great helpings of *cannelloni*, pasta with meat inside covered with a cheese sauce, to the members of her family who had come to dinner to welcome Kathryn and to discuss energetically the problems of Casare's amnesia.

'But he'll have to know she is coming, Mamma,' Cecilia had objected. 'The bus goes only to Molino. It doesn't go anywhere near the villa, so how is Kathryn to get there if Cesare doesn't drive into the village to pick her up?'

'I have thought of that,' Emilia had said with a twinkle of humour in her eyes. 'I shall phone Cesare tonight and tell him I have a woman to spring-clean the Villa for me. Last week-end when I was there I threatened him with a housekeeper, the place was in such a mess. I will tell him she will be arriving on the afternoon bus tomorrow and that he is to be there to meet her. I will also tell him she will be staying until the house is thoroughly clean and tidy.' Emilia had looked at Kathryn and had smiled conspiratorially. 'I'm sure you won't mind doing a little housework while you stay there, Kathryn?'

'No, I won't mind. But supposing Cesare doesn't recognise me when I get off the bus? Shall I tell him who I am?'

Immediately all the members of the family had talked at once, each one offering a suggestion. Bewildered as she had always been by such noisy family conferences, Kathryn had tried to listen to each one of them and had failed. In the end she had glanced appealingly at Vincente Vitelli, Cesare's father, the only one of them who hadn't so far offered her advice. At once he had banged on the table with his fist and the excited chattering voices had stopped.

'Tell him your name, your Christian name,' he had suggested, 'and see what happens then.'

'Supposing nothing happens? Supposing he believes she is really the housekeeper Mamma has sent?' Cecilia had demanded.

'Then I suggest that Kathryn goes along with that idea for a while and pretends she is the housekeeper,' Vincente had said quietly.

'You mean I shouldn't tell him ... I ... I'm his wife?' she had asked.

'*Si*, that is what I mean,' he had replied, and his dark eyes had looked steadily at her and she had felt the force of his strong will beating against hers. 'I believe we have told Cesare too much about what he ought to remember so that now he isn't sure any more whether he is actually remembering what is past or whether he is remembering what we have told him. We have been hoping that the return of this memory will be sudden, like a flash of light illuminating a dark room. But it is possible that won't happen. It is possible it will take even more time. Maybe only in living with you again will he remember what happened in that time before he crashed.'

Vincente had always been very kind to her, she thought now, as the bus glided down a hill towards the village. And so had Emilia. Even three years ago when Cesare had taken her to meet them for the first time their welcome had been warm.

Then they had been making a deliberate effort to hide their natural suspicion of the young foreign woman their beloved eldest son had married in such a hurry. They had been hiding their disappointment because he had not married one of his own countrywomen. For an Italian girl would have known how to be a proper wife. She would have borne him a child during that first year to cement the marriage. She would have known, because she had been brought up to know, that the responsibility for the stability of any marriage rests squarely on the woman's shoulders. She would have put family first and self last.

Yesterday they had again welcomed her warmly, and if they had felt critical of her because she had deserted Cesare they had hidden their feelings and had applied their ingenious minds to finding the best way for her to meet him again; a way that they hoped would result in the return of his memory and possibly in the restoration of his marriage to her.

The bus turned into a narrow street between the sun-gilded walls of old red-roofed houses where washing was hung out to dry on balconies. The yellow tassels of laburnum trees and the half-closed umbrella shapes of pines cast shadows over tiny courtyards seen through the railings of narrow gates hung between tall stone gate-posts. Ancient chimneys leaned in grotesque shapes above corrugated pantiles and brightly coloured shutters edged half-opened windows.

The street widened into a small piazza at the end of which a line of blue, red and green rowing boats bobbed on the water of the lake and nudged against a low wharf. The bus stopped in front of the shady colonnade of an old hotel just as the clock in the square bell tower of the church chimed five o'clock.

Following the three other people who were getting off the bus, Kathryn went down the steps into the warm sunshine. The bus driver took her suitcase from the luggage compartment and handed it to her. She thanked him and walked under the colonnade of the hotel away from

the bus so that she had a clear view of the piazza and so
that she could be seen by anyone who might be watching
for her.

Almost at once she saw the long, low Vitelli sports car.
Dark red in colour, it was parked in front of the church
under the shade of a flowering cherry tree. Should she
go over to it? No, better to wait for him to come to her.
In that way there would be more test of his memory.

The passengers who had got off the bus with her disappeared and the bus driver went into the hotel. All was
quiet in the sun-drenched piazza save for the cooing of
doves fluttering about the belfry of the church and the
sound of disco music coming from someone's radio.

Kathryn put down her case and paced a few steps in
the direction of the hotel entrance and back again to her
case. She didn't want to seem unduly interested in the
person who was sitting behind the steering wheel of the
Vitelli. He had to make the first move, come across to
her and ask her if she was the woman his mother had
sent to clean house for him. Or—ask her if she was indeed Kathryn, his wife.

The possibility of him doing just that caused sweat to
break out on her skin and her heart to quicken its beat.
Nervously she began to pace up and down again, wishing
he would hurry up and get out of the car, come across to
her. Surely he had seen she was the only person who had
got off the bus and had not left the piazza? Surely he
had studied her long enough, while pretending to read a
newspaper, to know she was the person he had come to
meet.

Reaching the doorway of the hotel, she studied the
menu pinned to a board outside, feeling suddenly hungry
as she read it. Apparently the hotel was known for its

bistecca alla fiorentina, charcoal-broiled entrecôte of steak. Behind her across the piazza she heard a car door slam, but she didn't turn. Instead she became interested in a poster which advertised that sailing dinghies were available for hire from the hotel and also speedboats suitable for towing water-skiers.

Limping footsteps sounded behind her and she stiffened a little. The family had prepared her for some changes in him. They had warned her that he limped and sometimes on bad days he was forced to use a walking stick. The damage to his spine had resulted in pinched nerves which had caused some paralysis of both legs. Through clever surgery and physiotherapy the paralysis had been partially cured, but he still felt a stiffness in his left leg. It was that stiffness, coming unexpectedly, and cramping the whole leg, which more than anything had prevented him from taking up racing again.

'*Mi scusi, signorina.*' He spoke behind her. Nothing different about his voice. It was still deep and musical, the product of living in a warm climate and speaking a musical language.

Kathryn turned quickly. He was just the same to look at—tall and broad-shouldered like his Lombardian father, black-haired and swarthy-skinned like his Roman mother, his dark green eyes set deep on either side of his big dominant nose beneath the jut of his powerful forehead.

The same, yet not the same, because his face was thinner, the lines of suffering carved permanently into the lean cheeks and across his brow. He was wearing a casual round-necked long-sleeved white sweat shirt and faded hip-hugging jeans. In his left hand he carried a walking stick on which he was leaning.

An expression flickered briefly in the dark eyes studying her and his forehead wrinkled in puzzlement.

'Forgive me,' he said. 'I have made a mistake. I am expecting someone from Milan, an older woman sent by my
mother to clean the house.' He smiled, that faint polite
curving of his well-shaped mouth which she knew so
well. It meant that although he didn't want to hurt your
feelings he had lost interest in you or in what you were
saying and he was going to walk away from you. She had
seen him do it so many times. It was the way he closed
his mind to any further impressions of a person he didn't
want to know any better.

Irritated because he was reacting in that way to her,
she said loudly and clearly to his half-turned back:

'I'm Kathryn, and your mother did send me to clean
the house.'

Slowly he turned to face her again. Again his forehead
wrinkled in puzzlement.

'Katryn, Katryn,' he repeated, and her heart missed a
beat. Was it possible he was remembering? He stared at
her intently. 'That is not Italian. We would use Caterina.'
His glance travelled over her neat shining hair, her
smooth face, down to the blazer jacket she was wearing
over a silky striped blouse and trim pencil slim skirt, right
down to her feet in high-heeled brown sandals. 'You
don't look Italian either. Are you from the border, from
the other side of the Alps? From Switzerland or Austria?'

'No, I'm English.' Maybe now it would come to him
who she was. Tense, braced for anything, she waited.
Again he frowned and this time teased with long muscular fingers the thick black curls which coiled closely to
his head.

'You speak very good Italian for an Englishwoman,' he
observed, flashing her a sudden underbrowed glance.

'I had a very good teacher,' she replied.

He had been her teacher. From the moment they had been married he had always talked in Italian to her, insisting it was the only way she was going to learn the language, and the times he had taken to trouble to give her special instruction had been some the happiest moments of their marriage, happening as they had when they had been alone either making love or waking from sleep or sharing a meal by candlelight in their apartment in Milan. Such precious happy moments they had been, and she hadn't realised how happy and precious until now when it was so obvious Cesare had no memory of them at all.

'I told my mother I didn't need a housekeeper,' he said abruptly. 'And if there was a bus returning to Milan tonight I'd suggest you go back there on it. But there isn't a bus until morning. So what are you going to do?'

Kathryn stared at him in dismay. This was something neither she nor any of his family had taken into account.

'Aren't you going to take me to the villa, then?' she stammered. 'I have to stay the night somewhere.'

'You could stay at the hotel. At this time of the year they have many vacant rooms. The tourist season hasn't started yet.'

'But. . . .' She broke off. How could she get around this stalemate without telling him she was his wife? 'I can't afford it,' she went on in a rush, and seeing scepticism glint in his eyes, she added quickly, behaving as she imagined someone whom Emilia had really hired to keep house might behave, 'I haven't any money at all. I spent the last I had on the bus fare. And if ... if....' She lowered her eyes, wishing she had the acting ability to squeeze tears from them and sniffed as if she were indeed on the verge of weeping. 'If I don't do as Signora Vitelli told me and go to the villa to clean it she won't pay me and then I'll have to look for another job. Please, *signore*, let me come and clean the house. I promise I'll keep out of your way. It won't take long, a week at the most.'

From under her long eyelashes she peeped up at him to see what effect her pleading was having on him. In the sunlight which slanted across it his face looked impressive, as if it had been sculptured from bronze, and his eyes were deep and dark as the green glinting water at the bottom of a well. She had never been able to guess what he was thinking and she couldn't guess now.

'You don't look as if you're short of money,' he drawled, his glance flicking over her insolently. Moving quickly, he snatched her handbag from under her arm before she could prevent him.

'How dare you!' she flared, going into action and reaching out to snatch it back from him, but he merely swung away from her and hooking his stick over one arm he opened the bag and took out her wallet.

'No money, eh?' he jeered, and flapped her wallet back and forth under her nose. 'Several thousand lire in notes and some coins, judging by the weight of your purse. You could afford more than one night in the hotel here.'

'Give me my bag!' she demanded, reaching for it again, but he backed away from her holding the bag behind him. There was nothing impassive about his face now. It was alight with devilry, a taunting grin creasing his cheeks and dancing in his eyes.

'Not until you stop pretending to be the housekeeper my mother has sent and tell me who you are. I want the truth now, no more play-acting, You're a rotten actress anyway,' he mocked.

Kathryn pulled up short, her eyes widening and her hand going to her dropped-open mouth. Then recovering herself she went right up to him and studied his face closely. He returned her stare steadily, his mouth slanting up at one corner in a mocking smile.

'You know who I am, don't you?' she accused.

'I think so. I think you're my wife, Katryn.'

Vaguely Kathryn was aware of the noise of traffic passing through the piazza, of people talking and laughing as they entered the hotel. The life of the village was going on all around them, yet she and Cesare seemed to be enclosed in a world of their own acting out a private drama under the arches of the hotel's colonnade, unnoticed by passersby.

'When did you remember me?' she whispered. 'Just now, when you first saw me?'

'I recognised you when you got off the bus, or at least I thought I recognised you.' Again his dark glance flicked over her curiously. 'There are differences. Your hair is different. I don't care for the way you have it. And you're wearing different clothes and seem thinner than in the photograph I have of you. You look older and more serious.'

'Oh!' She wasn't sure whether it was relief or disappointment which washed through her. 'So it's only from a photograph that you recognise me and not because you actually remember me.'

'Perhaps,' he murmured tantalisingly, and shrugged his shoulders.

'What is that supposed to mean?' she demanded.

'Perhaps it is only from the photograph and your name that I remember you because I know Katryn is the name of my wife and the photograph has written on it the name Katryn. But perhaps I do actually remember you. I have no way of knowing.' He shrugged again. 'Are you going to tell me now why you didn't say who you are but pretended to be the housekeeper sent by my mother?'

'It was your mother's idea. She thought it would be best if you didn't know I was coming to see you, a sort of shock tactic.'

'In the hopes that my memory would come back?' His mouth took on a sardonic twist.

'Yes. But I don't think they ... your parents and the rest of the family know you have a photograph of me.'

'You're right, they don't. I haven't told them.' He fastened her bag, handed it back to her and stared at her penetratingly. 'Is that the only reason you have come back, because they asked you to come?'

Kathryn looked away from him down at her handbag and fiddled with the clasp, remembering what Vincente had also suggested.

'Your father said that if I stayed at the villa with you for a while I might be able to help you to remember,' she muttered. 'But if you don't want me to stay there's nothing I can do about it, is there?' She glanced up quickly, but his face was devoid of expression as usual. 'I'd better go and see if I can book a room for the night in the hotel,' she added coolly, and swung round towards the hotel entrance.

'Wait ... Katryn.' He spoke urgently and she turned back to him. 'Haven't you forgotten something? Isn't that your case?' He lifted his stick and pointed with it in the direction of the case which was still at the far end of the colonnade.

'Oh, yes.'

She began to walk towards the case. To her surprise

he limped along beside her, and she felt a suddenly heart-rending anguish remembering how he had once moved, with graceful pantherish strides, covering the ground easily and swiftly.

They reached the case together and both bent to lift it. Cesare's fingers closed round the handle first.

'You'd better let me carry it,' she said, and tried to take it.

'Why?' he demanded, straightening up and swinging the case away from her.

'Because you might find it difficult to carry a heavy case when you have to walk with a stick to help you,' she replied, quite sincere in her wish to help him.

'Feeling sorry for me, Katryn?' he jeered softly.

'I don't want you to think you have to carry my case, that's all. I can carry it myself quite easily,' she said, trying to take the case from him again, and again he swung it away from her.

'Do you want to stay at the villa tonight or do you want to stay here?' he asked curtly, looking down at her threateningly.

'At the villa, of course, but you said....'

'I said that to get you to admit who you are,' he interrupted her. 'You can come to the villa because it's possible my father is right and that you might be able to help me remember what I've forgotten. But if you're going to stay with me you must hide any pity you're feeling because I limp. Is that clear?'

'Yes, but....'

'And be thankful I've offered to carry your case,' he added, his mouth tilting again in a self-mocking smile. 'I'm not always inclined to be chivalrous towards women. But you should know that.'

Yes, she did know that, thought Kathryn wryly as she
went with him across the piazza to the car. It had never
been his way to make an impression on a woman by being gallant and helpful. His approach had always been
much more direct and devastating. And he had always
been scornful of pity and sympathy. She should have remembered that, too.

He put the case in the back of the car, told her to sit
in the front and slid behind the steering wheel. The
elegant car glided smoothly into the middle of the plaza,
did a fast tight U-turn to face in the opposite direction
and turning left shot up a narrow hilly street as if it were
jet-propelled. Out of the village it roared along a road
which dipped up and down across a hillside terraced
with vineyards. The walls of an old farmhouse blushed
rosily in the rays of the westering sun and its windows
glinted gold. To the left the water of the lake shimmered
metallic blue between the purple-glowing cliffs of steep
headlands.

Kathryn glanced sideways at Cesare. He hadn't forgotten how to drive. Even with a stiff leg his reflexes were
remarkable as he changed gear swiftly and accurately to
adjust the engine to the different gradients and bends in
the road. It was difficult to believe he had been paralysed
for a while and that his memory refused to function.

'Have you driven along this road with me before?' he
asked abruptly, glacing at her out of the corners of his
eyes.

'Once. We came to visit your parents when they were
on holiday at the villa.'

'How long ago was that?'

'Two years ago, in June.' In spite of herself her voice
trembled a little as her own memory of that visit filled

her mind suddenly, and noticing, Cesare gave her another sidelong glance.

'Was it a good visit? Did we enjoy ourselves?' he demanded.

'Why do you want to know?' she parried.

'I'm conducting an experiment on myself. I'm trying to find out if there is anything in common with the parts of my life that I have forgotten.'

'Luigi told me you couldn't remember any of your past life that you don't want to remember beyond a certain point,' she challenged him.

'That was true for a while,' he conceded. 'But a few months ago the veil began to lift and I began to remember certain incidents, some from my childhood and some from my youth. For instance, one day when I was driving in the traffic in Milan I recalled quite clearly the first time I ever drove a car on my own.' A smile flashed suddenly across his face as he gave her another quick glance and she felt response to his attraction leap up in her. 'It was like doing it all over again,' he added. 'There was the same sense of excitement and achievement. After that I began to remember many incidents.'

'And people?'

'And people. Sometimes it happens in the early morning when I'm waking up. It's like being visited by the shadows of dreams,' he said softly. 'But you haven't answered my question. Did we enjoy that visit to my parents?'

Kathryn looked out of the side window at the lake. Soft dark blue shadows cast by the cliffs on the opposite shore were beginning to creep across the water to rob it of its bright sheen. From behind a mountain peak the disc of the sun peeped like a a half-closed eye, its radiance sparkling out in a blaze of reddish gold light.

The last time she had come along this road in the brightness of forenoon on a lovely day in June. How dark that day which had dawned so brightly had become later when, six months pregnant, she had tripped and had fallen down the staircase at the Villa Rosa.

'I lost our baby,' she said in a whisper. 'I had a miscarriage.'

The car swerved slightly and she looked round in alarm, but Cesare had the vehicle under control again. His face had gone very pale and muscles ridged along the angle of his jaw as his mouth set in a tight line of control.

'I'm sorry,' she said impulsively. 'I shouldn't have come out with it so ... so carelessly. I should have prepared you, led up to it. . . .'

'No, it's all right,' he said hoarsely, and took a hand off the steering wheel to rub at his forehead. '*Dio mio!* We were going to have a child? I hadn't remembered that, and no one told me.' He paused, his breath hissing between his teeth as he drew it in. 'That's been part of the trouble,' he added bitterly. 'The family, my mother, Luigi, Cecilia, the others, they have tended to avoid answering any questions I've asked them about our marriage, and that's the part of my life I don't seem to remember too well.'

Because you don't want to remember. Because you regretted being married to me. The suggestions were on the tip of her tongue, but she held them back. No point in telling him that yet. Time enough for her to make that sort of accusation when he had remembered more about their relationship, when he remembered how much he hated her.

'Were we glad we were going to have a child?' he asked.

'I was. I must have been because ... because I was so upset after losing it,' she muttered, and glanced away out of the window quickly, feeling tears well in her eyes. *God*, helping him to remember was playing hell with her emotions. How was she going to get through the next few hours with him, never mind the next few days, if remembering all that had happened between them was going to do this to her. 'I ... I'm not sure whether you were glad or not,' she added.

'Wasn't I upset too, when you lost it?'

'I don't know.' She said it flatly and coldly. 'You didn't say at the time and the next day you went away to take part in some races. They were important because they were in the championship series. You were trying to win the championship for the second year running. It was more important to you than....' Her voice quivered a little, so she paused and swallowed hard, continuing to stare at the lake. 'Naturally the championship was more important to you than I was,' she added bitterly. 'Your racing always came first with you, always.'

'Meaning you regarded me as a selfish swine, I suppose,' he retorted dryly. 'Is that why you left me?'

She turned quickly to look at him. His gaze on the curving road before him, he sat relaxed in the bucket seat, only the twist at the corner of his mouth betraying the nature of his thoughts.

'You know I did?' she exclaimed. 'You remember that?'

'I don't *remember* it, but I *guess* it. I haven't lost my intelligence just because I've lost my memory, you know. When I was told I had a wife but that she wasn't around to visit me it wasn't hard to figure out what had happened, and then when you didn't turn up at all....' He broke off and shrugged his shoulders. 'Have you done anything about getting a divorce?'

'No, I haven't. I ... I ... left that to you. You were in the position to file a suit. I had left you and not the other way round,' she answered sharply, and glanced away again at the lake. The sun had disappeared behind the mountain peak and although the sky was still flushed with a rosy glow shadows were beginning to creep across the water, darkening it.

The car went on steadily. Cesare didn't ask any more questions and Kathryn didn't look at him any more. For ten minutes they drove in silence with tension twanging between them. Then the car slowed down and looking round Kathryn saw they had reached the end of the narrow road which twisted up the hillside to the Vitelli villa.

Gravel chips crunched under the tyres as the car climbed the steep curve and stopped in front of an elegant three-storey house, built in traditional Italian style with a roof of red tiles, two rows of casement windows flanked by bright yellow shutters and a colonnade of stone arches over the front door and lower windows.

Birds hidden in the many shrubs and trees which clustered about the house were singing and the air was fragrant with blossom scent coming from the small grove of citrus fruit trees as Kathryn followed Cesare under one of the arches of the colonnade through the front door and into the house. This time she carried her case. He hadn't even offered to get it out of the car.

In the dim central hallway he turned to face her.

'I expect you remember the layout of the house,' he

said coolly. 'All the rooms on the first floor are ready for visitors. Choose whichever one you like to sleep in. I usually eat about eight o'clock in the evening. Do you want to eat when I do? Or would you prefer to get something ready for yourself earlier?'

'I'll eat when you do,' she said.

'In that case perhaps you won't mind doing the cooking. You'll find plenty of meat in the refrigerator and the usual selection of pasta in the cupboards. If you need anything and can't find it, I'll be in this room here.' He pointed towards a half-open door on his left and without another word turned and limped across the hall towards it.

Irritated by his cool arrogance and repressing an urge to tell him he could damn well cook his own evening meal because she had changed her mind and wanted to eat straight away, Kathryn stomped up the stairs to the first floor, intending to leave her case in the room where she would sleep and then to visit the bathroom.

She looked in all four bedrooms on that floor to find out which one Cesare was using. Judging by the unmade bed and the clothing which was scattered untidily about it he was sleeping in the back bedroom on the right-hand side of the stair-well, so she chose the front bedroom on the left-hand side of the stair-well to be as far away from him as possible.

The room was big and airy and overlooked the lake. It was furnished with hand-made pinewood furniture and a double bed covered in green and white striped cotton. After washing her hands and face in the bathroom Kathryn returned to the bedroom, unpacked her clothes and put them away and then taking some sheets from the bottom drawer of a chest of drawers she made the

bed, her mind busy going over the strange meeting with
Cesare outside the hotel.

Like her, he was different in some ways, a little older
than when she had last seen him, thirty years to her
twenty-four, his face marked by the pain he had suffered
during the past year, but he was far from being an in-
valid. She had imagined that loss of memory might have
made him subdued, possibly apathetic. How wrong she
had been! Essentially he was the same as he had ever
been; autocratic, proudly independent, quick to tantalise
her and provoke her into some form of retaliation, aware
of his own masculine attractions and not above using
them to get his own way with a woman....

Kathryn straightened the bedcover with a sharp tug
and then turned away to study her own reflection in the
mirror. So he didn't like the way her hair was and he
thought she looked older, and more serious. Well, she was
going to show him just how unimportant his opinion was
to her. She was going to show him too that he couldn't
get his own way with her, not any longer.

She went downstairs to the kitchen and stopped just
inside the door to gasp in dismay at the dirty dishes piled
high in the stainless steel sink, at the remains of a meal
on the round table. There was an unpleasant smell of
burn lingering on the air and the top of the modern
cooking range was cluttered with dirty pans and spat-
tered with blobs of cooking oil. No wonder Emilia Vitelli,
that most methodical and fastidious cook, had decided
that Cesare needed a housekeeper!

Her lips thinning in exasperation, Kathryn went back
through the door and along the hallway to the room into
which Cesare had gone. It was a library-study, lined with
bookshelves. Light from an architect's lamp attached to

the edge of a big desk dispersed some of the evening shadows and gleamed on Cesare's head as he bent over the desk. He didn't look up when she cleared her throat to attract his attention, nor did he say anything, so she marched right up to the desk.

'I can't cook a meal in that kitchen,' she announced coldly.

'Why not?' Still he didn't look up but went on writing down figures on the graph paper in front of him.

'It's in too much of a mess. How can you leave dirty dishes to pile up like that? And food out on the table? It's most unhygienic. I'm not surprised your mother thinks you need a housekeeper.'

'I'd have cleared it up eventually when I'd finished what I'm doing,' he replied calmly.

'What are you doing?'

'Designing a new racing engine for the company.'

'Couldn't you do that at the factory offices in Milan?'

'I do sometimes. Today I decided I could solve this particular problem better if I stayed here.'

'Why are you living here? Why don't you live in our ... I mean your apartment any more?'

'Because while I was in hospital learning to live again it was sub-let on a three-year lease. When at last I was able to leave hospital I was still having some problems with walking, so I went to live with my parents. As soon as I could get about on my own I moved out here. It's quiet and I can please myself what I do without anyone making a fuss.' He gave her an underbrowed glance. 'At least I could until you came. What are you going to do if you can't cook in that kitchen? Go hungry?'

'No, I'm not,' she snapped, feeling a familiar irritation rising within her because he was more interested in what he was doing than in her. 'But I do object to cleaning up a mess that's been made by someone else. And you have no right to expect me to.'

'I'm not expecting you to do anything,' he retorted coldly. 'You can do what the hell you like as long as you don't interrupt me when I'm working out a mathematical problem. Now, get out of here. We can talk later when we're having a meal.'

'And that's another thing. You've no right to expect me to cook for you just because we're still married,' she flared.

'Are you going to leave this room or do I have to carry you out of it?' he drawled threateningly.

'You couldn't,' she retorted.

'Couldn't what?'

'Carry me. Not with your leg the way it is. It took you all your time to carry my case,' she jeered.

His face went white and his eyes glittered angrily.

'You vicious cat!' he snarled savagely, lunging to his feet. He limped round the edge of the desk towards her, a threat in every uneven stride he made. 'What are you trying to do? Taunt me into laying hands on you? Is that what you want, Katryn? Some rough play?'

'No, it isn't.' She backed away from him, her hand reaching for the door knob. 'Right now, I'm wishing I'd never come to see you!' she added furiously, and stepping out into the hall she slammed the door shut.

CHAPTER FOUR

OUTSIDE the door of the study Kathryn stood hesitant, half expecting the door to be swung open and Cesare to appear, to fling more abuse at her. But the door didn't open and she wondered with a little flash of humour if he was standing on the other side of the wooden panels, breathless as she was, hesitating as she was, wondering whether to tell her to get out of the villa, never mind the room.

She was tempted to go. Only the thought of having to walk along the twisting road in the dark back to Molino was stopping her, she assured herself, as slowly she moved away from the door towards the stairs.

What was the use in her staying? She and Cesare had hardly been together an hour and they were bickering and backbiting in the same way they had those dreary weeks before she had left him.

On the other hand, what was the use in her leaving? Somehow he and she had to discuss the matter of their marriage and come to a decision, whether he remembered anything or not. With a sigh she turned away from the stairs and went towards the kitchen. Besides, she had to eat.

The pine-panelled walls of the kitchen gleamed golden under the glow of the electric light when she switched it on. It was a pleasant room, cleverly modernised to make the preparing of meals easy for the cook. It was a pleasant place to eat in too, when it was cleaned up.

She found an apron and put it on. Soon she was washing dishes and pan, rinsing them and stacking them to drain. That done, she attacked the cooker until it was clean and sparkling. Then she set the table, for two. Then she found some minced beef, onions and tomatoes.

As she chopped the onions for the meat sauce she intended to make to serve with spaghetti, she found herself remembering the times Emilia had shown her how to cook Italian recipes. And then with some surprise she found herself remembering how much she had enjoyed preparing and serving them for the candlelit dinners she had shared with Cesare in their apartment in Milan during the first year of their marriage.

They had had a lot of fun together at first. The physical attraction between them being very strong, she had always gone with Cesare when he had gone away to race. In fact for the first six months she had never missed watching him race, and even now she could remember clearly the odd moments of sheer joy she had experienced with him when, climbing from the cockpit of his car at the end of a race, he had always looked for her, had come straight to her to hug her, no matter who had been waiting to speak to him or congratulate him. He had liked her to be there and he had shown it.

Later when she had become pregnant she had not been able to go with him so often because she had suffered so much from morning sickness. She could remember feeling resentful because she had conceived. The possibility of having a child had never entered her head when she had rushed headlong into marriage with Cesare.

What a fool she had been, a silly immature fool, never thinking of the consequences of her impulsive action. But Cesare had been delighted when she had told him she was going to have a baby. So had the rest of the formidable Vitelli family. All suspicion of her had been wiped out completely when they heard the news. After all, Cesare was an eldest son and it was up to him to make sure the Vitelli family would continue to exist in the future by having sons.

'It is the best way to cement your relationship with Cesare,' Emilia had said one day, more to comfort than anything else because Kathryn had not been feeling very well and as a result had been resentful of her condition. 'Although here in the industrialised north and in the big cities the bad examples of other countries are being increasingly imitated by the younger generation. . . .'

'What bad examples?' Kathryn had interrupted to ask.

'Divorce, separation,' Emilia had replied.

'You think they are bad?'

'Of course I do. Anything which destroys a family is bad,' Emilia had retorted. 'In Italy the first source of power is the family, and it must be protected at all costs.'

'But supposing a woman and man who are husband and wife can't live comfortably together? If they are always quarrelling about something isn't it better that they should part?'

'Naturally it is desirable that husband and wife be happy in each other's company, but that isn't always necessary to make a marriage,' Emilia had replied. 'The principal purpose of marriage is not the impossible satisfaction of love dreams or the achievement of romantic ecstasy but the foundation of a new family and the reinforcement of existing ones.'

A little chilled by this practical realistic outlook, Kathryn had not been able to agree.

'Then supposing either of them is unfaithful to the

other. What then?' she had argued. 'Don't you think that's a good reason for divorce?'

Emilia had given her an ironic look and had shaken her head slowly from side to side.

'You have a lot to learn, my child, about the way we do things in this country,' she had said. 'We are very diplomatic people. If a husband or a wife is tempted to stray away from fidelity he or she or both of them must manage the affair discreetly so as not to hurt the other and consequently damage the structure of their marriage and so ruin the life of the family.'

'They must turn a blind eye, you mean?'

'*Si*, and a deaf ear,' Emilia had agreed with a chuckle.

'I don't think I could be like that if ... if ... I found out Cesare was unfaithful to me,' Kathryn had muttered. 'I would have to say something to him about it.'

'Then you would be making a big mistake,' Emilia had warned, very serious again. 'But it won't happen, Kathryn, because you are going to have a child. Let's hope it will be a boy, for no Italian man will do, without a great deal of hesitation and remorse, what many Englishmen, Americans and Frenchmen seem to do as a matter of course these days.'

'What is that?'

'He will not lightly abandon a wife who is the mother of his firstborn son.'

Perhaps that was why she had been so disappointed when she had lost the baby, thought Kathryn as she stirred the chopped beef into a mixture of fried onions, tomatoes and mushrooms. And how ill she had been afterwards, how depressed she had become when she had been unable to go with Cesare when he went abroad to race. Staying behind in Milan had not been good for her peace of mind. Knowing how attractive he was to women and knowing how much he enjoyed female company, she had grown suspicious and jealous and had subjected him to questioning about his activities when he had returned. At first he hadn't seemed to mind, but as time had gone on he had become very evasive and as a result they had begun to quarrel bitterly.

The kitchen door was pushed open suddenly and she looked round. Cesare limped into the room and across to the sink. He took one of the coffee mugs she had washed, turned on the tap and filled the mug with cold water. He drank all the water, rinsed the mug and put it back where he had found it. Then without a word, without a glance at her, he limped back towards the door.

The sound of his uneven footsteps grated on her nerves and pricked her conscience. Whirling round impulsively, she followed him quickly.

'Cesare, I'm sorry,' she blurted.

'Again?' he jeered, swinging round to face her. 'Why?' Hands on his hips, he stood looking down at her, his face set in hard unforgiving lines, and for the first time since they had met again she became aware of his powerful sensuality and she backed off a little.

'I shouldn't have said what I did about you not being able to carry me. It was a mean thing to say,' she said.

'But it was true.' His mouth twisted bitterly. 'You were right—I couldn't carry you without difficulty, not now.' He paused, frowned and rubbed at the corner of his mouth with a forefinger. 'Did I used to carry you?'

'Er ... yes ... sometimes.' Her glance wavered away from his dark intent one and to her irritation she felt her cheeks growing warm. Damn, she thought she had outgrown the tendency to give herself away by changing colour.

'When?'

'Oh ... er ... when we'd been fooling about some-times.'

'Fooling about? What does that mean?'

'We ... I ... you ...' She broke off, suddenly irritated by the way he was embarrassing her by his refusal to understand. He was doing it deliberately, she was sure, to tantalise her into telling him about incidents of their life together which she had tried so hard to forget. 'Don't you know?' she challenged with a lift of her chin.

Hands still on his hips, he studied her face and again she found herself wondering why it was she couldn't guess what he was thinking. After living with him for over a year, after knowing a man's body as intimately as she had known Cesare's, she would have thought she would have known something about the way his mind worked.

She drew a sharp shaking breath and hurriedly turned away from him, her heart thumping, her own body suddenly burning with remembered desires. Taking up a wooden spoon, she stirred the mixture of meat, onions and tomatoes, herbs and spices which was now simmering in a pan on the stove.

'I don't know, but I think I can guess,' he said with a lilt of amusement in his voice, coming across the room after her. 'It would start something like this, perhaps?'

His fingers were suddenly in her hair, dragging at the pins which held the topknot in place.

'No! Leave me alone, don't touch me!' she spat at him viciously, and swung out at him with the wooden spoon, spattering him with hot meat sauce. He withdrew at once and they stood facing each other, both breathing hard, eyeing one another like wrestlers before making a move.

Cesare shrugged, his mouth curved mockingly and his

eyes were hidden as he looked down at the blotches of tomato-coloured sauce on his sweat-shirt. He wiped them with his fingers, then touched his tongue to one fingertip to taste the sauce.

'Tastes good,' he commented. 'I thought you said you couldn't cook in this kitchen?'

'It's surprising what hunger will drive a person to do,' she retorted dryly. 'Would you like some? I've made plenty.'

'Are you by any chance inviting me to dine with you?' he asked with an ironic lift of his eyebrows.

'If you would like to,' she replied stiffly.

'I'd like to,' he said simply. 'I'll get some wine.'

When he came back to the kitchen twenty minutes later he had changed his clothes and was wearing a bottle green cotton open-necked shirt and trousers of pale gold velvet corduroy, the close fit of his clothing emphasising the breadth of his shoulders and chest and the lean muscular length of his hips and thighs. He had brought a bottle of Bardolino, that semi-sparkling red wine which goes with any meal, and after drawing its cork he put it on the table with two wine glasses.

Kathryn dished up the meal and they sat down at the table. Both being hungry, they didn't talk. As always Kathryn had difficulty in winding the long slippery skeins of spaghetti round her fork, so she was slow at eating. Cesare ate quickly as if he had been starving with hunger and then sat sipping wine and watching her.

'Please stop looking at me,' she protested.

'Stop looking at you. Don't touch you,' he drawled sardonically. 'You make being with you very uncomfortable for me. Was it always like this with us?'

She gave him a quick look from under her eyebrows as she wondered how to avoid answering the question.

'It's just that when you watch me all the time I find it hard to eat this. I'm not very good at winding it round the fork.'

'You never were.'

Again she flashed him another glance. A faint smile flickered about his mouth as he returned her stare.

'You remember?' she queried sharply.

'*Si*, I remember. I remember we often ate like this, the two of us by candlelight. What I can't remember is why we stopped doing it,' he said softly.

'There's plenty more spaghetti and meat sauce,' she said, her voice nervously loud. 'Why don't you help yourself to some?'

'You don't want to tell me, do you?' he accused, his voice still soft, his gaze still narrow and intent.

'Tell you what?' she countered uneasily.

'Why you left me.'

'Your father said you'd been told too much about your past life so that now you're confused and aren't sure what it is you actually remember and what it is you remember having been told. . . .' she began stiffly, but didn't continue because with an exclamation of irritation he got to his feet and picking up his plate went over to the cooker. The sound of his uneven footsteps pricked her conscience again and dropping her fork on her empty plate she sprang to her feet.

'I'm sorry, I should have got it for you,' she mumbled apologetically, sinking back into her chair as he came back to the table. Giving her an angry glare, he plonked his plate down on the table and sat down.

'Why should you?' he grated. 'And for God's sake stop

saying you're sorry every five minutes. I've told you I don't want your pity.'

'It isn't pity. I don't seem to be able to bear seeing or hearing you limp,' she confessed in a whisper.

'Don't you mean you can't bear the thought of being married to a cripple?' he jeered. 'Isn't that why you've taken so long to come and see me?'

'No, it isn't. I didn't know you'd been hurt until Luigi told me the other day,' she defended herself fiercely.

He frowned, finished scooping up his food, put down his fork and poured more wine for both of them.

'Where did he find you?' he asked.

'In Monte Carlo.'

Cesare paused in the act of raising his wine-glass to his lips and stared at her over its rim.

'That is where you and I met,' he said.

'Do you remember? Or did someone tell you?'

'I remembered ... right now, just when you said Monte Carlo.' A smile quirked his mouth. 'So it seems I make progress.' His glance flicked over her again. The faint smile faded and his face hardened. Suspicion glittered coldly in his eyes. 'What were you doing in Monte? Living with another man?' he demanded harshly.

'No, I wasn't! I haven't been ... wherever did you get such an idea?' she exclaimed angrily.

'It comes and goes in my memory whenever I try to remember what went on between you and me before you left,' he replied, staring down into his wine glass, the expression on his face morose and bitter. 'He's like a ghost haunting me all the time,' he added quietly.

'Who is?' she asked, with a little shiver.

'This man. And I have a vague feeling you knew him before I knew you and that possibly it was because of him that you left me, to go and live with him.'

Disturbed by what he was saying, her mouth suddenly dry, Kathryn picked up her wine-glass and swallowed the wine that was in it.

'Who is he, Katryn?' he persisted, leaning towards her across the table. 'Tell me and maybe I'll remember more.'

'I don't know, I haven't been living with any man. I've been working for a woman novelist. I've been her secretary for nearly sixteen months, now. I managed to get the job as soon as I went back to England. But I wrote and told you about it.'

'When?' he demanded.

'In April of last year.'

He closed his eyes and rubbed his forehead, his face set in lines of strain.

'April last year,' he muttered. 'What the hell happened in April last year?' He thrust the fingers of both hands through his hair to clasp his head and leant his elbows on the table to stare at her with tormented eyes. 'You wrote to me, you say. Then where is the letter?' he demanded hoarsely.

'I don't know,' she whispered, empathy with his tormented state of mind tearing her apart. 'Perhaps you didn't receive it. Perhaps you destroyed it.'

'What did you say in it?'

'I told you that I had a job and gave you two addresses you could write to if you wanted to contact me about ... about a divorce. You didn't answer it.'

He closed his eyes again, his face twisting as if he were in pain.

'I didn't answer it because....' he began softly, then swore suddenly and virulently and sprang to his feet. As he moved away from the table awkwardly his leg caught

against it, pulling the checked cloth. Glasses, wine bottle
and plates went flying to crash on the floor, but Cesare
didn't stop. He went on towards the back door.

'Cesare, what's wrong?' Kathryn demanded urgently,
going after him. 'Have you remembered something else?'

'*Si*, I've remembered something else,' he hissed between
set teeth, swinging round to glance at her as he wrenched
the door open. 'I've remembered why I crashed.'

He stepped outside and Kathryn rushed across the
room to follow him.

'Where are you going?' she shouted into the darkness,
but he didn't answer.

She ran outside, determined to follow him, but pulled
up short when she realised how dark it was beyond the
light which shafted out from the room behind her. She
wasn't sure of the layout of the area behind the house.
She wasn't sure, either, in which direction Cesare had
gone because she couldn't hear any sound of footsteps.

'Cesare, wait!' she called as she groped her way into
the gloom.

She collided suddenly with a wall over which some
sort of plant was growing. From the pricks she was re-
ceiving on her skin she guessed it was a rambling rose
bush. As she disentangled herself she heard the roar of the
Vitelli's engine starting up at the side of the house. Using
that sound as her guide and with panic lending wings to
her feet she found her way unerringly to the place where
the car had been parked.

'Cesare, wait, wait, don't go!' she yelled, but she was
too late. The car reversed in one fast movement and with
a screech of tyres leapt forward to charge down the steep
hill towards the main road, its red rear lights winking
balefully at her like two angry eyes.

For a few moments Kathryn stood still listening to the roar of the Vitelli as it went along the road in the direction of Molino. High above in a dark blue sky stars glittered brightly. Far below in the basin which had been gouged out of a rock by ice, millions of years ago, the lake shimmered occasionally with reflected starlight. In contrast to the daytime temperature the night air was cool, a reminder that here climate was affected by altitude.

The sound of the car was flung back to her in echo. It was going far too fast for that switchback of a road, its speed indicating Cesare's state of mind. What had he remembered to put him in such a rage and make him drive off like that, without explanation?

He could be killed. The thought made her shiver. Forgetting that the twisting road was not a racing circuit, he might collide head-on with a car coming in the other direction. He could be killed, and it would be her fault for coming here and trying to help him remember.

She shouldn't have come. She should have followed her first inclination to stay away. She shouldn't have let Luigi's remarks get under her skin. She shouldn't have let Constance persuade her. Above all she shouldn't have agreed to come alone to see Cesare; she should have asked Cecilia or Luigi to come with her.

What should she do now? What could she do? She would have to tell someone what had happened. She went back into the house by way of the kitchen. Glass and broken plates crunched under her feet and automatically she went to a closet, found a broom and began to sweep the mess into a dustpan, finding a certain amount of relief from her panic-stricken thoughts in doing something practical. By the time every bit of glass had been swept up and the wine which had been spilt had been mopped up she was feeling much more calm.

She cleared the table, washed up the utensils she had used for cooking, stored what was left of the meat sauce in the refrigerator. Tidying and wiping, her ears straining for the sound of the Vitelli returning, she came to a decision. She would do nothing for an hour and if Cesare hadn't returned by then she would phone the Vitelli house in Milan and tell his parents what had happened.

The hour passed very slowly as she sat in the comfortable lounge and tried to watch an Italian TV programme. Several times she thought she heard the sound of a car's engine and went to the window which overlooked the driveway to see if the Vitelli was approaching, but each time it was only a car going by on the lakeside road.

It was a familiar and distressing experience, this waiting for Cesare to come back. How many times she had sat like this during those few months before she had left him, waiting for him to come back from a race, worrying when he was late in case he had had an accident; wondering jealously if he were with another woman. It had been better by far to go with him and watch him race, even though that too had brought its own sort of worry, its own sort of jealousy. But at least she had been with him to see what was happening and to see that it wasn't another woman she had to share him with but a sport, the sport of trying to go faster than anyone else.

The programme she was watching came to an end. She looked at her watch. Over an hour had gone by since he had left and it was now ten-thirty. She would phone his parents. In the study she found a Milan telephone directory and was soon talking to Vincente Vitelli.

'Cesare has gone off somewhere, I don't know where,

in his car. He remembered something and it made him angry and I'm so afraid he might crash again. . . .'

'Did he tell you what he remembered?' Vincente's calm autocratic voice broke in on her rather breathless and worried explanation.

'He said he remembered why he had crashed.'

'But this is great news!' exclaimed Vincente. 'He didn't tell you where he was going when he left the house?'

'No, he . . . he just rushed out. I tried to stop him, but he wouldn't wait and. . . .'

'*Mi scusi*, Kathryn,' Vincente butted in again. 'Would you tell me, please, what you said to him just before he remembered?'

'I was telling him what I'd been doing, where I'd been working, and about the letter I sent to him in April last year. He asked me what was in the letter and I told him, and that was when he remembered.'

'But of course. It was in April last year the accident happened.' Vincente paused, then added, 'We did not know you had written to him, Kathryn. There was no letter from you among his correspondence at the apartment.'

'I know—Luigi told me. Signor Vitelli, I'm so afraid he might have another accident tonight. His leg is very stiff today and I think he's been in pain. . . .'

'Listen, my dear. The best thing is for you to go to bed and behave as if nothing unusual happened. I realise it is difficult for you, but there is nothing you can do. I think that possibly Cesare has gone to see someone who might be able to tell him whether what he has remembered is right. He might even be coming here. We'll let you know if he does. Now, try to relax, my dear. Go to bed, and sleep. He may be back sooner than you anticipate.'

Easier said than done, thought Kathryn when an hour and a half later she turned in bed restlessly, reached out and clicked on the bedside lamp to look at her watch. Twelve-thirty, and Cesare hadn't come back yet. The phone hadn't rung either, so presumably he hadn't gone to see his parents or one of his relatives.

She switched off the light and settled down to woo sleep again, but her thoughts kept revolving about the scene in the kitchen. Cesare believed she had left him for another man, someone she had known before she had known him. Was it possible he had known about her love for Tony? No, surely not. She had never mentioned Tony to him and at the races she had attended with him she had kept aloof from the British teams that had been entered. . . .

Except that last time when she had gone deliberately, had made herself go to find out whether her suspicions of Cesare were unfounded or not; to find out if he was indeed having an affair with Sophia Barzini or not.

She groaned and turned again, remembering how miserable she had felt on meeting the beautiful Sophia again. It had been then that she had realised how much she had fallen in love with Cesare. And ironically that had been the very time when Tony had sought her out, come to her to confide his troubles about his own marriage with Jane.

'It isn't working out,' he had told her as they had sat at a table in a small restaurant where he had taken her to dine one evening. She had gone with him because Cesare, who had had a run of bad luck with the car he was driving, had been busy trying to find out what was wrong with the engine so that it could be fixed for the race the next day.

'I'm beginning to think I asked Jane to marry me as a result of spring fever, that May in Monte,' Tony had continued. 'We were all affected by it. You and Cesare too.' His blue-grey eyes had held a curious enquiring expression. 'Remember?' he had prodded.

'Yes, I remember,' she had whispered, and had avoided his glance.

'You and Jane were always together, and I think I got mixed up,' he had said with his endearing grin. Then his face had sobered and he had added slowly, 'I proposed to the wrong woman, and now, seeing you again, being with you again, I realise I should have proposed to you. I'm in love with you, Kathryn.'

'No, no ... you can't be ... it's too late,' she had stammered in her confusion. 'We're both married and Jane loves you, I'm sure she does.'

'Does she?' he had retorted with an ironic lift of his eyebrows. 'Oh, she's possessive and jealous enough. You call that love?'

'It's difficult being the wife of a racing driver,' she had tried to defend Jane.

'I can't see that it's any more difficult than being the wife of a doctor or jet pilot or a train driver or a coalminer,' he had argued. 'They're all dangerous and demanding jobs.' He had looked across at her and had reached out to take her hand which had been resting on the table and had curled his fingers about it suggestively. 'But whoever said marriage is indestructible, Kathryn?' he had said insinuatingly. 'Or that its vows can't be violated?' He had laughed scornfully. 'And don't tell me Cesare did. We all know how he behaves when you're not with him.'

She had quivered as if he had stabbed her, but she

hadn't removed her hand from his because its strength had been all she had had to hold on to in that moment of crisis.

'Look at this evening,' Tony had continued. 'He's left you all by yourself.'

'There's something wrong with his car. He had to retire from today's race,' she had muttered.

'And you really believe he has to be there when the mechanics work on it tonight?' he had jeered. 'Oh, come on, Kathryn, you know better than that.'

'He always liked to be there. You know he's as much interested in the mechanics as he is in the racing. It's his knowledge of engine design which helps him to be such a good driver,' she had argued.

Tony had laughed again incredulously and had shaken his fair head from side to side.

'Those Italians,' he had drawled derisively. 'How subtle and devious they can be! Or to put it more bluntly, how good they are at lying and cheating. Cesare is probably dining right now with Sophia Barzini in her hotel room. She's followed him about Europe all summer.' His hand had tightened on hers and he had given her a suggestive glance. 'Let's go to my room now, Katie darling.'

'No!'

'You know you don't mean that, my sweet.'

'Yes, I do. I don't want to go to your room. I don't want to make love with you.'

'You did once,' he had accused, and she had glanced at him in surprise. 'Oh, yes, I know how disappointed you were when I asked Jane to marry me. I remember how pale you went, how you managed to avoid congratulating us, how you got up and rushed into Cesare's arms,' he had taunted.

Staring at him, she had wondered why she had ever been attracted to him, for at that moment he had seemed a cold, cruel presumptuous devil.

'I didn't rush into his arms,' she had retorted, and had managed to remove her hands from under his. 'He asked me to dance with him.'

'And you made the most of it, didn't you?' Tony had jibed. 'And when he asked you to sleep with him you refused. You blackmailed him into marrying you.'

'I didn't! That isn't true!' She had risen to her feet.

'Isn't it? You don't really believe that Cesare Vitelli would have proposed marriage if you'd been willing to oblige him without, do you?' he had sneered. 'I remember how surprised we all were that you and he had eloped. How we laughed because someone as young and innocent as you were then had managed to bring the Great Lover to his knees. . . .'

With an exclamation of distress Kathryn had turned away and had hurried from the restaurant and had gone back to the hotel suite she had been sharing with Cesare. To her relief Tony hadn't followed her and eventually she had gone to bed and had waited for Cesare to come, as she was lying awake and waiting for him now.

But he hadn't come. He hadn't slid into bed beside her and taken her in his arms, so she had come to the conclusion that Tony had been right after all and that Cesare, tired of her, had been with Sophia.

Next morning when she had gone into the sitting room of the hotel suite she had been surprised to find Cesare, still dressed in shirt and trousers, fast asleep on the couch. He had woken reluctantly when she had touched his shoulder and had lain there blinking up at her in the bright sunlight.

'What time did you come in?' she had asked.

'About five o'clock,' he had replied drowsily, his eyes beginning to close.

'Why didn't you come to bed?'

'I didn't want to disturb you,' he had yawned.

'It would be the first time you hadn't wanted to do that,' she had retorted sharply, and his eyes had opened wide. The next second he had been laughing. Reaching up, he had put his hands to her waist as if to pull her down on top of him.

'Did you miss me?' he had mocked softly. 'Then let's make up for what we both missed during the night, here on this couch, my lovely Katryn.'

'No!' She had stepped back out of his reach.

'So you need some persuasion, hmm?' he had said with a grin, and with a quick movement he had been off the couch and standing in front of her with his hands fanning over her breasts. His lips had burned the tenderness of her and for a few seconds she had given in, parting her lips willingly, her breasts swelling and hardening to the caress of his fingertips.

Then it had come to her that he might have been kissing some other woman like that, probably the sultry-eyed, poppy-mouthed Sophia Barzini, and she had experienced a violent feeling of revulsion. Wrenching her mouth from his, she had pushed away from him.

'What's the matter?' he had asked, his voice ominously quiet and his eyes beginning to glitter in a way that warned her his temper had been on the short side that morning.

'I don't know where you've been all night,' she had muttered evasively. 'You could have been anywhere with anyone.'

'Of course you know where I've been,' he retorted, his face hardening with exasperation. 'I told you I'd be supervising the work which had to be done on the engine of the car.' He had thrust a hand wearily through his hair and had turned away from her to look out of the window. 'It took much longer than we had expected, and even now....' He had shrugged fatalistically. 'I don't think I'm going to make the championship this year.'

'I don't believe you,' she had said.

Cesare had turned to face her again. His face had been wan with sleeplessness and dark lines had been scored beneath his eyes. There had been the slump of disappointment in his broad shoulders.

'What do you mean?' he had asked with a puzzled frown. A faint smile had flicked about his mouth and again he had pushed the hair back from his forehead. 'Forgive me, I do not feel very bright this morning. I need more sleep.'

'I mean I don't believe you spent all night supervising the work done on the engine,' she had said, and his temper had exploded.

'God, I'm tired of this!' he had fumed. 'Tired of your suspicion and your jealousy!'

'And I'm tired of your lies....'

'Lies?' he had exclaimed, striding over to her and glaring down at her. 'When have I lied to you?'

'You're always doing it, pretending you've been busy with the cars, sending Luigi or one of the others to tell me you'll be late, making excuses....'

'Katryn, *carissima*.' Again his voice had softened and he had stroked the hair away from her neck. 'I'm sorry I had to leave you by yourself last night. I had hoped it would be different, that we could have gone out together and danced like we used to do....'

'Stop it, stop it,' she had whispered, stepping back from him. 'I can't bear it any longer. I can't bear it when you pretend to love me knowing that you don't, knowing you love another woman.'

'What other woman?'

'Sophia Barzini.'

'Sophia?' he had exclaimed, frowning at her with hard eyes. 'What do you know about her?'

'Enough to make me wish I'd never married you.'

He had gone very pale, but his shoulders had straightened proudly and he had looked at her down his nose.

'So what are you going to do about it?' he had challenged. 'If you don't like being my wife any more why don't you do what you're always threatening to do? Why don't you leave me?'

For an awful moment Kathryn had stared at him, scarcely able to believe her ears. Then her pride had come rushing up. Tossing her head so that her hair had swung back behind her shoulders, she had moved past him on her way to the door of the room.

'Maybe I will,' she had retorted coolly. 'I'm going for breakfast now.'

'And I'm going to bed,' he had growled.

She hadn't been able to eat much breakfast; she had been too upset. After several cups of coffee she had gone back upstairs to the suite and straight into the bedroom. Cesare hadn't been in bed as she had expected. He hadn't been anywhere in the suite. He had gone out again without telling her where he had gone, treating her once again as if she were of no account.

It had been then that she had decided to take him at his word and leave. She had packed her few clothes quickly. Only when she had been in the lift going down to the lobby had she remembered the signet ring and had

decided to leave it at the reception desk. She had called
a taxi and had driven to the local railway station where
she had taken the first train back to Milan. By evening she
had been on another train bound for Paris on her way
back to England.

Kathryn sighed and turned over again so that she was
facing the window. At last she was beginning to feel
drowsy. Next minute her eyes were wide open and she
was tense again as she watched a shaft of light shift across
the window pane like a searchlight. Then it was gone.

Sitting up, she listened intently. Yes, there was the deep
throb of the Vitelli's engine as it idled. It stopped and all
was quiet. Then a car door slammed. Relief gushed
through Kathryn and she lay down again. Cesare was
back.

There was the muffled distant sound of a house door
being opened and closed. A long silence. Light leapt suddenly across the bottom of the bed from the partially
open doorway of the bedroom and the stairs creaked as
someone crept stealthily up them. Uneven footsteps
crossed the landing floor. The light streaming across the
bed was blocked by something in its way.

Kathryn let her glance slide to the doorway. Cesare was
leaning against the jamb looking in. She didn't move and
she didn't speak. He straightened up ready to move. Her
heart seemed to stop and start again with a bump and she
felt suddenly very hot. A floorboard creaked. Light
streamed directly on to the bed again. He had gone away.
A door opened and the landing light went out. All was
silent except for the pounding of her heart, and she wondered vaguely as she slipped into sleep why disappointment mingled so strangely with relief.

CHAPTER FIVE

KATHRYN groaned out loud. Her head twisted from side to side on the pillow. She muttered something unintelligible and then called out quite clearly :

'Cesare, Cesare! Oh, wait for me, Cesare!'

There was a roaring sound in her ears, a mixture of engine throb and people's shouts. She was rushing along at great speed and everything was changing shape and colour rapidly about her. Bright lights flashed and flags fluttered. She was in a kaleidoscope, caught in one of those tubes of coloured glass which as it turned blurred the reflections of everything seen through the glass.

No, that was wrong. She wasn't in a kaleidoscope at all. It only seemed as if she were because everything was going by so fast. She was sitting at the steering wheel of a car, its wheel hard and cold under her gripping fingers. She looked down. She was wearing a pair of the maroon red Vitelli racing overalls and on her head there was a protective helmet. She was driving round a racing circuit!

The car in front of her was coming very close. It looked very strange, like an overgrown insect, close to the ground, its wheels outside the chassis, not under it, and a sort of wing at its rear. Frantically she searched for a brake lever with her left foot, but there wasn't one. She tried to spin the steering wheel to alter course, but it wouldn't turn.

Then the car in front disappeared and suddenly she was out of her car and standing on the edge of a precipice looking over and seeing the other car hurtling over and over through the air, going down and down until she could hear it no more. And someone was screaming.

'Cesare, Cesare!' That was her voice speaking. 'Cesare, where are you?' she called.

'Here, beside you,' he said softly in the darkness, and she turned on to her side, reaching out an arm, curving it about the solid warm bare body which lay beside her in the bed. She put her head on his shoulder. It felt good beneath her cheek, hard and smooth.

'I'm glad you've come back,' she whispered sleepily.

'I'm glad I've come back too,' he replied.

'I thought you'd crashed again. I saw you crash.'

'You were dreaming.'

'Oh! Am I dreaming now?' She was disappointed again. Cesare was always disappointing her. Sometimes she thought he did it deliberately as if he was trying to get his revenge on her for something she had done to him.

She moved her hand, and rough hairs crisped beneath her palm. They felt real enough. Her fingertips slithered upwards in exploration and tangled in the thin chain. Groping further, they found and felt the round disc of a medallion, the Saint Christopher medallion she had once given him. Someone sighed.

'You are here, then, in bed with me?' she whispered.

'*Si*, I am here in bed with you.' Laughter shook the deep voice and she felt the heat of his hand against her waist, stroking its curve intimately, before it slid round to her back. It was a comforting hand and it pressed her closer to him until her hipbones touched his and the tips of her breasts tingled against the hardness of his chest.

'You called out my name in your nightmare.' His

breath moistened her forehead. 'So I came to you.'

'You drove over the edge of the precipice. It was horrible, horrible!' She was shuddering suddenly from head
to foot with the aftermath of the dream. His arm tightened about her and he whispered to her in Italian, soft
sweet silly words, designed to soothe and comfort her.
Against her temple his lips were warm and soft. They
moved over her cheek and hovered tantalisingly close to
her mouth.

'Forget the dream,' he said. 'I'm here, alive and beside
you. This is reality.'

'Yes,' she mumbled, and settled her head more comfortably against him. Luigi had been right, reality was better
than any dream or romantic imagining. Contentment
flowed through her relaxing all tension and she fell asleep.

Morning sunshine was flushing the sky with golden light
when Kathryn opened her eyes again. Swallows twittered
as they swooped in under the eaves of the house to build
their mud nests where they had built them every year
and a faint breeze coming in through the slightly open
casement window lifted the green and white striped curtains.

Sitting up, Kathryn looked about her. She was alone in
the bed and the room looked exactly as it had been when
she had switched the light out last night. Her dressing
gown was where she had left it, draped over a chair, and
there were no other clothes about; no man's pyjama
trousers tossed down on the other side of the bed.

She frowned. She felt very heavy-handed as if she had
slept too long and the remnants of strange dreams kept
flickering through her mind. A car hurtling over the edge
of a precipice. Herself screaming for Cesare. His voice

speaking to her softly and comfortingly. His hand at her waist, against her back, his lips touching her cheek.

Fingers against the cheek she imagined he had kissed, Kathryn shook her head sharply, hoping to clear it. If she had dreamt that Cesare had been in bed with her perhaps she had also dreamt that he had come back last night. Certainly everything was very quiet, as if the house was empty.

She swung off the bed. The frill edging the long skirt of her nightdress frou-froued about her feet as she went over to the chair and picked up her blue velour dressing gown. She pulled it on and tied the belt. Leaving the room, she went barefooted along the landing to the room Cesare had been sleeping in.

The door was open. She pushed it open further and looked in. The room was in much the same state it had been in the day before. Clothes were everywhere, the bed was unmade and on top of the crumpled sheets and blankets were the men's pyjama pants she had expected to see in her room.

There was nothing to point to the fact that Cesare had come back and had slept in that bed. She could have dreamt it. Outside the room she paused and listened. She thought she could hear the murmur of voices, so she hurried downstairs and went towards the study room. Yes, there was someone in there. A voice, masculine but not Cesare's, was speaking.

'When did you call to see Sophia?' it said.

'Last night. I left a message there to be passed on to you,' Cesare replied, and Kathryn breathed a sigh of relief. She hadn't dreamt he had returned. He was really in this house. She had only dreamt the other part, that he had been in bed with her.

'So you think you've remembered what happened at Barcelona last April and you want to know if anyone in our pits saw what happened,' said the other man, with a strangely mocking inflection in his voice. 'Would you mind telling me what it is you remember?'

Kathryn missed Cesare's reply because she was just absorbing the sense of the first words she had heard. Cesare had gone to see Sophia last night. He had been with that woman, not with her. So nothing had changed. Instead of staying with her and telling her what he had remembered so suddenly about the crash he had gone to Sophia. Didn't that prove that he still loved the woman, and turned to her instinctively for reassurance?

Jealousy clouded her mind, distorting her view of everything and curdling her feelings until they burst out beyond control. Her hand went out to hit the panel of the half-open door. The door swung open and she entered the room quickly as if pushed from behind.

Cesare stopped speaking. Two masculine heads, one covered with crisp black curls, the other covered with smooth dark brown hair, elegantly barbered in the latest masculine style, turned. Two pairs of eyes, one dark and unfathomable, the other pair light grey and surprised, stared at her. Then both pairs of eyes changed, became insolently appreciative, making her aware of her appearance, of the low neckline of her dressing gown and of the nightdress beneath it, the tangled curls and waves of her hair floating about her flushed cheeks, the bareness of her feet.

Slowly both men rose politely to their feet.

'Katryn.' Cesare's voice was like it had been in her dream, deep and a little amused. '*Permetto che le presento*

—may I introduce you—to Mario Ganzetti? Mario, this is Katryn—my wife.'

Kathryn flashed a glance in his direction. He hadn't forgotten who she was, then. His gaze travelled slowly over her again and his eyebrows went up slightly, enquiringly, as if he wondered why she had burst in on them while still in her nightwear. Then the other man was speaking and she had to turn to him.

'*Buon giorno, signora,*' he was saying. Tall and slender, he was wearing a well-tailored suit of grey pinstriped material with a navy blue shirt and pale silk tie. His face was long and narrow, just saved from being smoothly handsome by a slightly crooked nose. His narrowed grey eyes smiled right into hers before he raised her proffered hand to his lips to kiss it gallantly. 'I am very pleased to meet you at last,' he murmured as he released her hand. 'I have heard so much about you.'

Kathryn's eyes flickered in Cesare's direction again. Standing behind the desk, leaning against it slightly, he was watching Mario Ganzetti and there was an unpleasant twist to his well-shaped mouth, almost a sneer, as if he didn't care for the other man's smooth, polished manners.

'You have heard about me from Cesare?' asked Kathryn, speaking in English because Mario had used that language.

'No, from my cousin, Sophia Barzini. You and she have met, I believe.'

'Yes, we have.'

'But Sophia did not tell me how ...' he broke off and made a helpless gesture with his hands. 'I am not sure how to say it in English. She did not tell me how charming ... no, that is not right ... how lovely, as fresh as a newly-

opened flower, you are. But then perhaps she has not
seen you when you have just risen from your bed.' His
glance swept over her again in sensual appreciation and
Kathryn's hand went to the place where the deep lapels of
her dressing gown crossed over and pulled them together.
Pink colour bloomed faintly in her cheeks, but she managed to return his gaze coolly.

'There is no need for you to speak to Katryn in English, Mario,' Cesare said cuttingly. 'She understands
Italian perfectly well and speaks it too. She had a good
teacher.'

He had sat down abruptly behind the desk and a frown
of pain marred his handsome face. Or was it a frown of
disapproval? Kathryn wondered. Certainly he looked
very stern, like his father could look sometimes. She had
never seen him look like that before.

From under his frowning eyebrows he gave her a cold,
dismissing look.

'Did you want to see me about something?' he asked
quietly.

'I ... er ... I wondered if you'd had breakfast yet,' she
explained, turning to face him, aware that Mario had
moved politely away to look out of the window.

'Si, I have had breakfast.' His mouth curved sardonically. 'About two hours ago. It is now eleven-thirty. You
slept well and long, my so lovely wife.' His glance raked
her. 'May I suggest you go and get dressed? Don't forget
why you're here, will you? To clean the house for my
mother. She phoned earlier and said I was to tell you not
to bother with the third-storey rooms but to start with the
back bedrooms on the first floor and work downwards to
the ground floor, leaving the kitchen to the last. She says
she hopes you will do a good job.'

A glint in the depths of his dark eyes mocked her as she glared at him, irritated by the irony in his voice. He knew as well as she did that the job that Emilia had been referring to was not housework but the restoration of his memory and possibly the restoration of their marriage.

'I'm not sure I can stay any longer,' she retorted in a low voice, giving a quick glance in the direction of Mario's polite back.

'Why not?'

'Living with you hasn't changed. You still go off without explaining where you're going. You still stay out half the night.'

'You were worried about me?' Again he seemed amused, his mouth curving in a slight smile although his eyes were hidden as he looked down at the blueprint of an engine design which was on the desk.

'Of course I was.'

'Why were you?' He looked up sharply.

'Anyone would have been, the way you went off last night,' she evaded. 'I'm not going to stay here to go through another night like that,' she added, turning away.

He muttered something and she swung round again.

'What did you say?' she hissed.

'*Che peccato*. What a pity.' He was smiling again, that secretive smile at his own derisive thoughts.

'What is a pity?'

'That you don't want to go through another night like last night. When and how will you leave?'

'Today, when Signor Ganzetti goes.'

'I see.' He gave her a slow up-from-under glance, a strangely menacing look in his eyes which sent apprehension quivering along her nerves. 'But you are not leaving dressed like that, I hope,' he added dryly, his glance drift-

ing to the exposed cleft between her breasts. 'Go and get
dressed properly and make some lunch for us.'

'I'm not here to make meals for you,' she hissed at him.

'Why not? You're my wife, aren't you?' he taunted.

'Meaning my place is in the kitchen, I suppose.'

'Among other places, yes,' he drawled, his gaze rov-
ing over her again in that subtly suggestive way, 'Now,
your hair is the way I remember it,' he murmured pro-
vocatively. 'Leave it that way, *per favore*, at least while
you stay here.'

'I shall do it the way I want it, to please myself and
not to please you,' she retorted, and swinging round
marched out of the room. Up the stairs she stormed to
her room and slammed the door shut.

Going over to the window she leaned on the sill. The lake
was placidly blue under the arch of a blue sky and on the
opposite shore which faced the midday sun a thick forest
of mixed trees shimmered brilliantly green. In the distance mountains, some sharply pointed, some softly
curved, were purple or lavender, laced with silver and
gold according to how the sunlight slanted across them.

The scene, so lovely and serene, calmed her nerves. She
collected her toilet bag and went along to the bathroom
and turned on both taps in the wash basin. Water spurted
in a series of noisy rushes from the hot tap, but none
came out of the cold tap. Then the hot tap began to gurgle
ominously and the water stopped altogether. Kathryn
frowned, then turned off both taps and left the bathroom.
Intending to go to the study to ask Cesare what had happened to the water system, she paused, glancing down at
herself. No, she wasn't going into that room again to risk
the blatantly sensual stares of the two men. She would

ask him later. Now she would have a quick wash in the small amount of water which had come through, dress and then pack her clothes ready to leave when Mario Ganzetti left. As for preparing lunch for Cesare and the other man ... well, she supposed she could do that. She had to eat too.

She dressed quickly in the pencil-slim skirt and striped blouse she had worn the day before. Surveying herself in a long mirror, she changed her mind about wearing them since the weather seemed very warm and put on instead a full cotton skirt made from gaily-flowered material and a plain amber-coloured, collarless blouse which buttoned down the front.

She brushed her hair and was about to sweep it up into its chignon when she remembered what Cesare had said about it. Immediately she was swamped by memories of him making love to her, sliding his fingers through her hair, burying his face in it, sniffing it and even tasting it while he had told her how much he loved its silkiness its fragrance and its colour, silver as moonlight. Even last night he had. . . .

Last night he hadn't been with her in bed. He hadn't come to her when she had screamed in nightmare. He hadn't taken her in his arms or kissed her gently or stroked her hair. She had dreamt it all. Last night he had visited Sophia. She had heard Mario Ganzetti say so.

There was something familiar about Mario and about the name Ganzetti, she thought, as forgetting about packing her clothes she left the room and went downstairs. Yet she was sure she hadn't met him before. If they had met he would have said so, wouldn't he? And she was pretty sure she wouldn't have forgotten his sort of suave elegance or that he was a cousin of Sophia's.

She went into the kitchen. It was full of sunlight. To her surprise it was also tidy. Cesare had washed up the dishes he had used from breakfast and had left them to drain. There was a newspaper on the table, folded back to a sports page. One of the headlines caught her eye. *GANZETTI WINS AGAIN OVER VITELLI*. Pulling the paper towards her, Kathryn sat down and began to read.

'Ever since an accident in the early spring of last year robbed the Vitelli team of their brightest star, Cesare Vitelli, everything has gone smoothly for Giuseppe Ganzetti. Time after time he has succeeded in beating the other Vitelli entrants in Grand Prix races. Neither Luigi nor Giulio Vitelli have their elder brother's dedication to the sport nor indeed his understanding of the complicated machinery which they are handling. At the moment of going to press Ganzetti reigns supreme also in the production and sale of sports cars to the élite, a field once dominated by Vitelli.'

Kathryn pushed the paper aside. Now she knew why the name Ganzetti was familiar. The Ganzettis and the Vitellis had been rivals for years, each family trying all the time to go better than the other in a typical Italian-type feud, like the Montague and Capulet families in the old story of Romeo and Juliet, only instead of fighting and duelling with one and another in the streets they confined their battle for superiority to the racing circuits and the car salerooms of the world.

But she hadn't known that Sophia Barzini was a Ganzetti before her marriage. Knowing that snippet of information now made it easy to understand why Sophia's parents had interfered and had prevented her from marrying Cesare. Possibly the Vitelli parents had disapproved too.

She found the apron she had worn the night before and tied it on. Picking up the kettle, she went to the sink and turned on the cold tap. A small stream of water spurted out of it then stopped with a gurgling sound. She turned the tap open further. A little more water glugged out, turning into a drip which soon stopped all together.

Why wasn't there any water? And where did the water supply for the villa come from? Kathryn realised she hadn't the slightest idea, having taken it for granted that it came from the waterworks and was piped into the house in the same way water was supplied to houses in a city.

Turning off the tap, she left the kitchen and went along to the study. Mario Ganzetti was just leaving the room, closing the door after him. He strode purposefully towards the front door and swung it open. Kathryn hurried forward.

'Signor Ganzetti, are you leaving so soon? I thought you would stay for lunch.'

Hand on the doorknob, he turned to face her. His long narrow face was set in hard lines and his light eyes flickered with an angry expression. As soon as he saw her his expression changed. He smiled and once again his glance roved over her admiringly.

'I regret, *signora*, I shall have to forgo that pleasure,' he replied politely, and glanced at his wrist watch. 'I have to attend a meeting in Milan this afternoon and it is time I was on my way there.' His eyes narrowed calculatingly. 'Have you been here long?'

'Since yesterday,' Kathryn replied, stepping out into the colonnade and letting the front door close quietly behind her.

'Are you hoping for a reconciliation, you and Cesare?'

Mario asked, and when she glanced at him sharply made a gesture with his hands and turned the corners of his mouth down. 'It is well known that you and he have not lived together for some time now.'

'No, that isn't why I am here,' she said coolly as they moved together from the shade of the colonnade into the sunshine towards the bright blue compact Ganzetti car which he had parked in front of the house. 'I came only because the family asked me to come. They hoped that a meeting with me might trigger off his memory.'

'Oh. Indeed?' He seemed indifferent. 'And has it?'

'Yes. Last night he remembered why he crashed in that accident.'

'Mmm, so he was saying.' Mario opened the front door of his car, then looked down at her, a slightly pitying expression on his face. 'I'm afraid it is not his memory working, but his imagination. I was present at the race in which he crashed. I saw what happened, and I believe it was caused by mental aberration on his part. He was not thinking what he was doing. Apparently he was in a very strange mood just before the race—had some sort of an argument with one of the other drivers.' Again he gave her a slyly admiring glance from under his eyelids. 'Sophia is not going to be pleased when she hears you are staying here with him alone.'

'I'm not staying. I'd like to leave today, but I have no car.'

'Where do you want to go?' he asked.

'Milan would suit me very well.'

'Then of course I shall be delighted to have your company if you're ready to come now,' he replied.

'Thank you. Could you wait a few minutes while I pack my suitcase?'

'*Si*, I'll wait for you. You are going back to Tony? How is he?'

'You mean Tony Baxter?' she exclaimed.

'I do. Last time I saw you you were with him in a restaurant in Monza. You were holding hands.' His smile deepened and his glance swept over her knowledgeably. 'I remember I told Sophia later about seeing you and him together, and she was very interested.'

'No, I'm not going back to Tony, as you put it,' she replied stiffly, returning his suggestive glance coolly. 'I haven't seen him since that evening.'

'Really?' He didn't bother to hide his disbelief, shrugged his shoulders as if he had lost interest and glanced at his watch again. 'Would you mind hurrying with your packing, *signora*? I can't wait very much longer.'

Kathryn went back into the house and upstairs again. Ignoring the puzzled questions which were clamouring inside her demanding answers, she began to take clothes out of the closet and fold them into her case.

She had to admit she wasn't attracted to Mario Ganzetti and she hadn't liked his remarks about herself and Tony. So he had told Sophia, had he, about seeing her with Tony? And Sophia had been interested. Kathryn's heart jolted and she stopped what she was doing. Dry-mouthed and wide-eyed, she stared at the skirt she had been folding. Was it possible that Sophia had told Cesare?

The sound of a car's horn bleeping outside was an ultimatum, urging her into action. She pushed more clothes into her case and closed it. Slinging a cardigan about her shoulders, she went over to the dressing table and inspected her handbag, making sure everything she needed was in it. It was no use her staying, she kept telling herself. No use at all. Cesare was still involved with Sophia and while he was there was no place for herself in his life, so she had best get out of it . . . again. She had been a fool to come, a silly romantic fool. . . .

As she lugged the heavy case along the landing she felt hunger twinge in her stomach and hoped that Mario would stop somewhere on the way for lunch. Down the stairs she lumbered and had to pause at the bottom to put the case down for a moment because carrying it was making her left arm ache. Changing her handbag over to her left arm, she was picking up the case again when she heard the unmistakable sound of a car starting up.

As fast as she could she crossed to the front door which was conveniently open, went through it and pulled up short to stare as the Ganzetti car disappeared down the driveway. Of all the arrogant, impatient men she had known, Mario Ganzetti topped the list! she decided crossly. Dropping the case on the path, she kicked it to relieve her feelings. If it hadn't been so heavy she might have got downstairs faster.

'Don't take it out on the case.' Cesare spoke mockingly, and Kathryn whirled round in surprise. He was leaning against one of the stone pillars of the colonnade. He pushed away from it and limped towards her.

Hands thrust into the front pockets of his jeans, he stopped in front of her. His collarless, close-fitting dark blue body shirt was slit down the front almost to his waist and against the smooth olive skin of his powerful neck the silver medallion chain glistened in the sunlight. From beneath drooping black lashes his eyes gleamed at her mockingly.

'I told Mario you had changed your mind about leaving with him,' he drawled.

'Oh, you. . .!' Kathryn kicked out at him, but he stepped back quickly and her toe didn't make contact and she had to be content with showing her annoyance by stamping her foot on the ground. 'You had no right to do that!' she flared.

'I think I have,' he retorted arrogantly. 'I don't like the idea of my wife consorting with a man like him.'

'Consorting?' She nearly choked on the word. 'I was only going to ride in his car. That's hardly consorting with him.'

'You'd have been in his company for several hours, and I couldn't allow that.'

'Really?' she gasped. 'I can't believe it!' She shook her head from side to side incredulously. 'I just can't believe it. You and I have been separated for nearly eighteen months and. . . .'

'There was no legal separation,' he interrupted her forcibly, and stepped towards her again, towering over her as if he wished to dominate her by sheer physical power, and it was her turn to step backwards, afraid of close contact with him. 'We were only separated because you stayed away from me,' he added.

'Well, you didn't make any effort to invite me back, did you?' she retorted.

'How could I? I didn't know where you were.'

'And didn't try to find out,' she snapped back. 'And now I've hardly been here a day and you start behaving like . . . like. . . .' She broke off and shook her head again, laughing mockingly. 'It's incredible!'

'I start behaving like a husband. Is that what you were going to say?' he taunted.

'Yes. A medieval one,' she jibed, tossing back her head to look up at him challengingly. 'What are you going to do now? Punish me for committing the sin of asking another man to give me a lift in his car to Milan where I can catch a train or a bus which will take me on my way to Monte? Are you going to lock me up?'

'I can't,' he replied practically. 'There are no locks on the doors in this house.' He shrugged his shoulders and turned away from her. 'You can leave if you want to. I didn't want you going with Mario, that's all.'

'Why? What do you have against him?' she demanded, following him, and he swung back to her.

'This,' he said tautly. 'No man's wife is safe with him.'

'Oh, I see. Double standards,' she jibed.

'What the hell does that mean?'

'It means that like a lot of men in this country you have double standards. It's all right for you to have an extra-marital liaison with another woman, but your wife mustn't wander from the straight and narrow. I can't go for a ride in the car with Mario Ganzetti, but you can associate with his cousin Sophia. You can visit her and stay half the night with her.'

'How do you know I visited her last night?' he demanded.

'I heard him say so just before I went into the study.'

'You eavesdropped?' he accused scornfully.

'I did not! I couldn't help hearing what he said. So you can't lie, you see. You can't deny you went to see her.'

'I admit I went to her house. I was hoping to see Mario there—he was a spectator at the race when I crashed. I thought he might be able to tell me whether what I remembered yesterday evening was right. He wasn't there, so I left a message for him. That's why he came out here this morning.' He moved towards her again. 'Katryn, I didn't stay half the night with Sophia,' he said softly.

'From her house I went to see my father, then I came back here. I was going to tell you all about it when I came in, but you were asleep.'

'You were very late. I was tired,' she muttered.

There was a tense silence. Kathryn turned away from him, but his hand on her arm prevented her from going back to her case. She flashed him a surprised glance. His expression was very grim.

'We've been through all this before, or something like it, haven't we?' he said bitterly. 'We've quarrelled over Sophia?'

'You remember?' she exclaimed.

'*Si*, I remember,' he drawled, his mouth twisting. 'I remember everything.'

Turning, he went into the house. Kathryn stood staring after him, nibbling uneasily at her lower lip. She looked down at her case. She could leave if she wanted to, Cesare said, as long as she didn't leave with Mario Ganzetti. And now she knew why he had said she could leave. What the Vitelli family had wanted to happen had happened—the meeting with her had triggered off his memory. He had remembered how much she and he had quarrelled before she had left him. He had remembered, and now he was hating her.

But she couldn't leave unless he drove her into Molino for the bus and before she left she would have to have something to eat, she was so ravenously hungry. Going to the case, she picked it up and staggered with it into the hallway. She left it by the front door and went down the hall into the kitchen. The sight of the twinkling stainless steel taps reminded her about the lack of water. There was nothing else for it, she would have to tell Cesare.

The study door was open, so she walked right in. He

was sitting at the desk again with his head resting on his hands as he studied the drawings in front of him. Hearing her, he looked up and across at her. The smouldering hostility in his dark eyes seared her like a red-hot poker might have done and she flinched a little.

'What do you want now?' he asked curtly.

'There's no need to make it so obvious,' she objected.

'Make what obvious?'

'That you wish I hadn't come to see you and make you remember things you don't want to remember. I didn't want to come, and I wouldn't have come if your family hadn't been so insistent,' she said defensively.

'You think I haven't realised that?' he snarled savagely.

'I'd leave now, only I can't walk all the way into Molino carrying that case and ... and I haven't had breakfast yet.'

'I told you to make lunch,' he replied, more coolly, and looked down at the drawings again.

'I know you did. But I can't cook anything. There isn't any water.'

Cesare looked up again, his eyes narrowed and suspicious.

'You're sure?'

'Of course I'm sure. I've turned on the taps and nothing comes out.'

His breath hissed between his teeth as he drew it in in exasperation. Pushing back his chair, he stood up and came round the desk. He was limping again and using the desk as a support, resting one hand on it.

'I'll get your stick,' said Kathryn, noticing it was propped in the corner by the doorway. Taking hold of it, she offered it to him as he came towards her. He snatched it from her and tossed it away from him. It clanged against a wall and slid to the floor.

'I'm trying to manage without it today, thank you,' he said crossly.

'But your leg is stiff and it ... it ... hurts you to walk,' she whispered, empathy because he was in pain once more tearing her apart.

'I don't need you to tell me that,' he said, his lips twisting viciously. 'I've been sitting too long. I'm supposed to exercise it more ... without the stick. But you don't have to stay around to watch me limp.'

He pushed past her and went out into the hall, turning in the direction of the kitchen. Kathryn followed him. He went straight to the sink unit and turned on the taps. Nothing came out of them, so he turned them off.

'Where does the water came from?' she asked.

'Each villa has its own private supply from the streams which come down the hills or from wells. We get ours from a stream. Something must have disturbed the pipe or blocked it. Maybe the filter has come off the end of it and some stones or even a trout have got into it. It has happened before,' he said. 'I'd better turn off the pump or it will burn itself out trying to pump up non-existent water to the taps.'

He opened a door and disappeared down some steps. Kathryn went to the door and looked down a flight of stairs leading into a basement. She heard Cesare moving about, then he reappeared and came back up the stairs. He limped over to the back door and swung it open.

'Where are you going now?' she asked urgently, remembering how he had left the previous evening without telling her where he was going.

'Up the hill to examine the end of the pipe,' he replied curtly, and stepped outside.

Kathryn hesitated for a moment, then rushed into action, walking quickly out of the house. She caught up with him in the grove of orange trees. Sunlight was warm and yellow and the fragrance of blossom was all about them as she put a hand on his arm to hold him back.

'Cesare, you can't climb the hill,' she protested.

'Why not?' He frowned down at her.

'Because ... oh, because of your leg.'

'I can manage,' he retorted stiffly, shaking her hand off and moving forward.

'I'll come with you,' she insisted, catching up with him.

'You don't have to.'

'But your leg....'

'Look, will you stop pretending that you care about what happens to me?' he snarled viciously, turning on her. 'We both know you don't care and never have. I don't need your help to fix the pipe. I don't need you. Go away. Leave me alone!'

He turned away from her and began to walk up the hill following the narrow path across the grass in the direction of the stream. Drawing a deep breath, Kathryn tried to ignore the pain which sliced through her at his rejection of her and, squaring her shoulders and gritting her teeth, went after him, reaching his side when he stopped at the edge of the stream.

He squatted down and plunged his hand into the clear sparkling water.

'What are you doing?' she asked.

'Checking that the water pipe isn't broken where it goes underground. It goes under the orange grove from

here to the basement. It seems to be all right.' He withdrew his hand from the water and shook it dry, then said,
'The rest of the pipe goes upstream to a pool in the gorge
higher up the hill. The pool is never empty even in the
driest of summers because it is fed by a spring.' He stood
up and slanted a mocking glance at her. 'I'm going up
there now.'

'And I'm coming with you.'

'Persistent, aren't you?'

'Only because I care. Very much.'

'You didn't when I married you.'

'What makes you think that?' she retorted, but was
unable to hide her surprise at his accusation.

'I told you I remembered everything,' he drawled
dryly, then added sombrely, 'I don't think I'd really forgotten. I'd had difficulty in bringing everything which had
happened between us into clear focus, that's all. Last
night it was as if an electric light clicked on in my mind
when you mentioned that letter. I remembered reading
it before going off to race. I shoved it in my overalls
pocket. It must have burned when they caught fire and I
remember. . . .' He broke off, his face hardening. 'I remember everything,' he repeated. 'I remember you married me because you were hurt when Tony Baxter
proposed to your cousin Jane instead of to you.'

'Who told you that?' Kathryn gasped.

'I didn't need to be told—I guessed. You married me
on the rebound.' He shrugged. 'Nothing new in that.'

'But if you guessed I was in love with Tony why did
you ask me to marry you?' she whispered.

'Who knows?' Again he shrugged. 'You and the night
and the moonlight went to my head, I suppose. Nothing
new in that, either.' His mouth curled bitterly again. 'My

guess about you and Tony was confirmed when you and he revived your affair after he had split with Jane.'

'We didn't revive any affair. We didn't have one to revive,' she protested.

'Have you forgotten what happened at Monza?' he jeered. 'Everyone saw you and him holding hands in a restaurant and I wasn't surprised when you left the next day.'

'But I didn't leave because of Tony. You dared me to leave. You didn't want me any more because your beloved Sophia had come back,' she accused tremulously.

'So we come back to Sophia again,' he said with a touch of humour. 'We've come full circle, haven't we, and are back at the point when you left me. Where do we go from here, Katryn?' he challenged.

'I don't know. I thought we could talk it out in a civilised way,' she suggested hopefully. 'Perhaps while we're having lunch. Do you have to fix the pipe? Couldn't we get enough water for cooking from here, in a bucket?'

'You could if you had a bucket.'

'I'll go back to the house and get one.'

She turned and ran back through the orchard to the house. It didn't take long for her to find a bucket. Swinging it at her side, she hurried back to the stream. Cesare wasn't there, and she looked up the stream. Trees crowded closely about it and it was impossible to see whether anyone was walking up the hill beside it, but she guessed he had gone up to the pool.

He didn't need her help. He didn't need her. He wanted her to go away and leave him alone—by going off without her he had underlined the message. Presumably he didn't want to discuss their relationship over lunch either.

Kneeling down, she dipped the bucket in the stream and lifted it out when it was full of water. Slowly she lugged it back to the house. She might as well make lunch for herself only. After all, she was very hungry. When she had eaten she would decide whether to stay another night or whether to ask Cesare to drive her into Molino.

CHAPTER SIX

Too hungry to take the time to prepare the usual three-course midday Italian meal of soup, meat and fruit dessert, Kathryn scrambled eggs for herself and made some coffee. She sat and ate at the table under the window from which she had a good view of the orange grove and the hill rising behind. As soon as Cesare appeared she would see him.

She couldn't help feeling anxious about him now that she knew he remembered everything. He even remembered why she had married him, and that was something she hadn't realised he had known. He had known about Tony and now remembered she had been seen with Tony eighteen months ago in Monza. Was that why he had told her to leave him?

She gulped down the last of her coffee, rose from the table and took her dishes to the sink. While she washed them she wondered what she should do next. There was so much explaining to be done by herself and by Cesare before they could even begin to discuss the question of divorce, and it would have to be done now his memory had returned. She couldn't go back to Monte as she had intended to earlier. There could be no more running away for her; she would have to face up to the reality of the situation and so she would have to wait for him to come back from the hill.

The sunlit silence of the house oppressed her. She wandered into the study and out of it again. She must find something to do, so she would start on the house-cleaning. It was going to be difficult to do without running water, but she could begin by tidying up the room which Cesare was using.

The room had a good view over the orange grove and up the hill, so as she collected up clothing either to hang it up in the closet or to toss it into the dirty clothes basket on the landing she was able to keep a look-out for Cesare.

When she had re-made the bed with clean sheets and tidied everything away she went downstairs, intending to fetch more water from the stream and bring it into the house to heat in the kettle. Across the grove she wandered back to the place where she had collected water before and where she had last seen Cesare. She filled the bucket, put it down at her feet and stood listening.

The only sound was the tinkle of water rushing over rocks. No birds were singing on that warm spring afternoon and no leaves rustled. No voice called down from the higher slopes either, yet she had this prickling sixth sense that Cesare was in trouble and needed her help.

He had been gone almost two hours, so she had better go to look for him. Leaving the full bucket beside the stream, she began to walk up the hill. At first it was easy because there was a well-defined path, but after a while the path disappeared under tangled undergrowth which pricked her bare legs. Fallen trees blocked the way and had to be climbed over. Several times she had to cross the stream by way of stepping stones because the way was clearer on the other side.

At last she came to a wide basin in the rock of the hill. A twinkling cascade of water fell over the high far side of the basin into a deep green pool. Kathryn paused to wipe the sweat from her brow. This must be the pool Cesare had mentioned. Cupping her hands about her mouth, she shouted his name as loudly as she could, hoping her voice would carry beyond the rushing sound of the little waterfall.

'Cesare, where are you?'

'Here.' His voice speaking behind her made her jump. Whirling round, she scanned the sunlit glade of birch trees and grey outcrops of rock. He was lying there, his shoulders resting against the silvery trunk of a tree, the picture of a man taking his ease on a warm sunny afternoon; a man without a care in the world, while she had been worrying herself sick imagining him either senseless, knocked out by a fall or groaning in agony.

'What are you doing?' she demanded, walking across to him. Under the sunlight his thick black curls were shiny, glinting here and there with blue light as he tipped his head back to look up at her.

'Resting, sleeping, dreaming a little,' he replied coolly. 'What are you doing here?'

'I'm looking for you. Don't you realise you've been up here for more than two hours?'

'I'm surprised you've come. I'd have thought you'd have left by now, gone back to your novelist in Monte Carlo,' he drawled, easing himself on to one hip and propping his head up with his hand. Selecting a long piece of grass, he pulled it and began to chew the milky white stalk.

'I can't leave—I told you why. I can't walk all the way to Molino,' she said, gritting her teeth.

'You could have phoned the hotel there and asked for a taxi to come out for you.'

'But I didn't know there was a taxi service.'

'You could have found out by looking in the local telephone directory.' He gave her a mocking sidelong glance. 'That is if you really wanted to go,' he added.

'I've been waiting for you to come back,' she retorted, and went closer to him. 'Cesare, we've got to talk.'

'Have we?' He lay on his back again, arms akimbo, fingers laced behind his head supporting it. 'That's the trouble with women, they're always talking, talking or wanting to talk. *Yak, yak, yak,* analysing everything, wanting to find motives for everything. My mother, my sisters, you—you're all the same,' he drawled tauntingly, and closed his eyes. 'I would rather not talk right now.' He opened one eye to look at her. 'Why don't you lie down too, rest after your climb up the hill? You're all out of breath.'

His eye closed again and Kathryn stood for a moment seething inwardly, half tempted to turn round and go back down the hill and do as he had suggested, phone the hotel and ask for a taxi. But to do that wouldn't solve anything, urged a new voice within her, the new grown-up Kathryn who didn't run away from reality but faced up to it and came to terms with it.

So she sank down on the grass beside him, tucking her legs beneath her, supporting herself on one arm and also plucking a long grass to chew. The place he had chosen was in full sunshine. She could feel the heat warming her face and penetrating the thin stuff of her blouse. Taking off her damp canvas rope-soled shoes, she wriggled her toes in the sunshine to dry them and looked sideways at Cesare.

He was steaming! Turning fully so that she could see him properly, she stared at the steam which was rising like a thin mist from his jeans and his shirt. His clothes were wet and were slowly drying in the sun. His feet were also bare and the running shoes he had been wearing were lying side by side also steaming.

'Men talk too,' she taunted back. 'All the time about cars and engines and winning, about how clever they are at fixing things like water pipes and about how they don't need any help, especially if it's help from a woman. How did you get so wet?'

'I had to wade into the pool to find the end of the pipe,' he murmured, not opening his eyes.

'Right up to your chest?' She peered closely at his hair. Yes, it had been wet too and the sheen on it was dampness. 'Right over your head?' she added scornfully. 'The pool is so deep?'

He didn't move nor did he open his eyes, but she had the impression he had tensed.

'It is deeper than usual because of the run-off from the melting snows higher up,' he replied smoothly. 'I was right about the pipe. The filter had come off. The run-off would have caused that too and the pipe was blocked with stones and a small trout. I had to find the filter and put it back on the end of the pipe when I'd cleared it, otherwise the flow of water would have been blocked again. Naturally I got very wet, and I thought I'd dry out here before going back to the house. The sun is warm and it's very peaceful here.' He paused, then added quietly, 'You didn't have to wait for me to come back. You could have left if you'd wanted to.'

'I couldn't go, not before I ... I ... was sure ... I mean, before we had discussed the situation,' she muttered.

'What situation?'

'Our situation,' she ground out between her teeth.

'You didn't seem to think it was necessary to do that when you decided to go with Mario.'

'That was before I knew you'd remembered everything.'

'It makes a difference, hmm?' His voice was lazy. 'My remembering everything?'

'Of course it does. Cesare who told you that I dined with Tony that night at Monza. Sophia?'

'No. Luigi told me.'

'But he wasn't in the restaurant.'

'I know. He was with me helping with the work which had to be done on my car.'

'Then how did he know?'

'Someone told him, I forget who. After you had left I asked him and some of the other drivers if any of them had seen you. He told me then that you had been seen with Tony the night before, behaving in a very friendly way. Tony hadn't turned up for the race that day and it was discovered that he had checked out of his hotel about the same time you had. I assumed you'd gone together.'

'But I didn't go with him. I had no idea he'd left Monza. I went to Milan, packed up and went straight to England.'

'But not to your uncle's and aunt's home.'

'How do you know?'

'Because I contacted them. Your aunt had no knowledge of your whereabouts.'

'I went to see Jane first,' she muttered.

'Why?'

'I thought she might put me up for a few nights. We were good friends once and I thought I might be able to help her patch up her marriage with Tony. I made a mistake,' she said, her voice still low. 'She told me to get lost, said she never wanted to see me again. She said it was my fault that her marriage to Tony was breaking up. She wouldn't listen to me when I tried to explain.'

Cesare turned his head to look at her with eyes which were slitted against the brightness of the sunlight.

'What did you do?' he asked.

'I found a room in a women's hostel in London and began to look for a job. By the end of the week I was employed by Constance Dale and went to live in her home near Brighton. Soon afterwards she decided to move to Monte Carlo and I moved with her.'

'Why didn't you write and let me know where you were?' he demanded gruffly, leaning up on his elbow again and shading his eyes with his hand against the sunlight.

'I ... I ... tried several times ... but each time I tore the letter up,' she mumbled, looking away from him. His movement had brought him quite close to her and his head was on a level with her shoulder. Her hands tingled suddenly with a desire to touch his face, run fingers through his clustering curls, and pull his head against her breast. 'I didn't think you'd be interested,' she added weakly.

'Dio mio, you were arrogant,' he accused tautly.

'Arrogant?' She swung round to look at him, offended by the accusation. Arrogant was a word she had never heard applied to a woman before. It was men who were always arrogant.

'Si. You took for granted I wouldn't be interested in knowing where my wife had gone. You behaved with complete disregard for my feelings and without any consideration for those of my parents. Did it never occur to you that we would all be anxious about you when we couldn't find out where you had gone and why?'

'But ... but I left you a note and your signet ring,' she argued. 'Didn't you get them?'

'*Si*, I got them.' He sat up properly, bending one leg cautiously to get his balance and leaving the other one, the left one, stretched out straight. 'Now what did that note say? Ah yes, I remember.' His mouth curled sardonically. 'It went something like this: "I can't live with you any more. Our marriage is over. Goodbye." Very clear, very dramatic, but not very informative, don't you agree?' he added mockingly.

'I was upset at the time,' she retorted, tilting her chin. 'You say I didn't consider your feelings when I left you. Well, let me tell you this. Never once did you consider mine during the time I lived with you.'

'You think not? And so you ran away to punish me?' He gave a short laugh. 'A child's trick,' he scoffed. 'You were hoping perhaps I would run after you? Then you should have left a forwarding address so that I would have known where to find you, shouldn't you?' he shrugged, and shifting position again lay back on the grass, carefully stretching both legs before him. Kathryn thought he looked very pale and there was a deep frown between his eyebrows.

'Your leg is hurting you, isn't it?' she said softly and sympathetically, leaning over him, but withdrawing when he gave her a glittering hostile glance.

'A little,' he admitted grudgingly.

'You shouldn't have walked all the way up here,' she said. 'Can't anything be done to relieve the stiffness and the pain?'

'I am doing something. I attend the hospital three days a week for physiotherapy. I spend hours with the leg in traction,' he replied curtly.

'Couldn't you have an operation to relieve the pressure on the nerve?' she asked.

'I suppose I could.'

'Then why don't you?'

'Have you any idea how many operations I've had in the past nine months?' he growled at her. 'I'm tired of having operations.' He turned his face away from her, shading it with one hand. 'I wish to God I'd died when I crashed,' he muttered on a note of suppressed violence. 'I wish I'd gone up in flames with the car.'

'No, no, Cesare, you mustn't say that,' she cried urgently, shifting on to her knees to lean over him again.

'Why mustn't I?' he retorted, turning to glare up at her. 'What good am I like this? I'm helpless. I can't do the things I want to do. I can't race a car any more. I can't even do a simple job like fixing a water pipe ... without ... without....' He broke off to mutter virulently under his breath and his eyes closed and the frown of pain creased his forehead again.

'You fell, didn't you?' said Kathryn. 'I knew it would happen. I knew I should have come with you to help you.' She leaned over him further, peering at him anxiously, and touched his face tentatively, her hand curving along the angle of his jaw. 'Cesare, tell me what happened, please,' she whispered.

He raised a hand to take hold of her wrist and his eyes opened slowly.

'I'm glad you didn't come with me. I'm glad you weren't there to see me falling in the pool. After I'd fixed the pipe I made for the bank again, but my leg cramped up and I fell. I managed to get up again, but it kept giving way under me,' he told her. 'I wouldn't have wanted you to be there to see me floundering about like a stupid. . . .' he began to call himself rude names and she moved her fingers from his jaw to press them over his lips.

'Shush!' she ordered. 'I won't have you putting yourself down like that.'

'You'd have pitied me,' he muttered, his eyes glittering menacingly at her through their thick lashes.

'No, I wouldn't. And I wouldn't have thought any less of you because you fell,' she asserted sincerely. 'But . . . but I might have laughed at you,' she admitted.

His hands tightened on her wrist and she felt his lips move against her fingers in a light caress before he lifted them from his mouth. He looked up at her with eyes which were suddenly very dark and soft.

'I remember the way you used to laugh at me and make fun of me,' he mused. 'It gave me a good excuse to. . . .' He paused tantalisingly and his glance went to her mouth.

'To what?' she whispered, leaning closer, her heart hammering against her ribs and filling her ears with its excited thunder as the heat of desire swept through her, weakening her limbs.

'To stop your laughter like this.'

He slid a hand through the thickness of her hair. His fingers pressed against the nape of her neck. With a little sigh she lay against him, her breasts growing taut against the hard feel of his chest. Their lips touched tentatively at first, then clung hungrily.

The skin of his throat was cool and slightly damp under her caressing fingers and his gasp of pleasure at the gentle pressure of her thumb against the hollow behind his ear lobe filled her mouth with his breath to mingle with hers. His lips hardening with roused passion bruised the softness of hers so that she moaned in an agony of pleasure and her fingers tugged hard at his crisp black curls in retaliation.

Taking his lips from hers, he lay back and looked at her, his eyes half-closed, his hands warm against the skin of her waist beneath her blouse.

'This is how I remembered being with you, when I was lying in the hospital. The memories would come in the night to torment me. Images of a woman with hair which looked like spun silver in the sunlight. I'd remember the way you smelt and tasted and the way you would tantalise me when you were in a wild mood. I'd remembered the softness of you lying against me, the way you would quiver when I touched you like this.' His thumb moved over the hardened point of her breast. 'And your body would become boneless and seem to melt into mine, and mine would melt too as you moved your hands over me.' His breath came out in a sigh of longing. 'Do it, now, Katryn, *per favore*, make love with me.'

Her senses reeling under the intoxication of his soft seductive voice and the tender touch of his hands, Kathryn lowered her lips to his again and let herself drown under the flood of passion which swept through her. The sun beat down on the couch of grass where they lay entwined, lacing their skin and hair with golden light, but its heat was no stronger than the heat of their desire for each other after so long a separation.

'Did you always purr when I stroked you like this, little lioness?' Cesare whispered against her throat, as his hand slid up her bare thigh.

'As much as you groaned and trembled when I stroked you like this,' she replied, slipping her fingers inside the waistband of his jeans to stroke his stomach.

'So we were good together?' he asked, moving away from her a little so he could see her face.

'Don't you remember?' she taunted.

'Now I do, now I am with you, like this.' He drew her down against him again, holding her there with one arm across her back while his lips claimed hers again demandingly. 'I want you, *carissima*,' he whispered against her mouth. 'I want you so much it is hurting like hell.'

Hands pushing against his shoulders, she wrenched her mouth from his, rolled off him and twisted to her feet. Shaking all over with the effort of resisting him, she glared down at him as he pushed up on his elbows and frowned at her in puzzlement.

'What is the matter?' he asked.

'Are you sure it's me, the person who is me, you want?' she demanded. 'Wouldn't any woman do?'

'*Non capisco. Cosa vuol dire?* I don't understand. What do you mean?' he asked, sitting up and supporting himself with his arms stretched behind him. 'Why would I want any other woman when you are here? You're my wife and....'

'And so you think you can take me whenever you want,' she accused. 'Just because you feel like it. Just because you want a woman!'

She bent and pulled on her canvas shoes with some difficulty because they had shrunk a little after their immersion in the stream. When they were on she tucked her blouse into the waistband of her skirt and tried to smooth her hair as she looked across at Cesare. He was still sitting in the same position watching her with a faintly sardonic smile lifting one corner of his mouth.

'What about you?' he scoffed softly. 'Didn't you want to take me? Just because you felt like it. Just because you want a man. Any man?'

'No, that isn't why....' She broke off, turning away from him in case he saw the truth of her feelings betrayed in her face.

'Then why, Katryn? Why return my kisses? Why fondle me so seductively if you weren't trying to turn me on? And why, for God's sake, pull away at the last minute? Are you still trying to punish me, because Tony has never come up to your expectations?'

'No!' Again the negative exploded from her and she swung back to glare at him again. 'Oh, why do you go on so much about Tony?'

'Because he's between us. He's always been between us,' he drawled rather wearily. Holding on to the slender trunk of birch sapling, he was getting to his feet slowly, every movement expressive of pain. Once he was upright he leaned against the tree, hands behind his back. Looking up into the sunlit, freshly green leaves, he laughed. 'That's why I punched him when I got your letter suggesting a divorce,' he added.

'You hit Tony?' she exclaimed.

'Sì. Before the Grand Prix race at Barcelona in which I crashed. He looked very surprised with the blood spurting out of his nostrils, but I didn't have time to explain. The race was about to start.'

Kathryn stared at him in consternation, remembering what Mario Ganzetti had told her about Cesare being in a strange mood before that race, having an argument with one of the other drivers and crashing because he had suffered from mental aberration, his mind hadn't been on what he had been doing. He hadn't been concentrating on driving. He had been thinking about her letter. Did that mean she had indirectly been the cause of his crash? Oh, God, if that were so how could she live with the burden of it on her conscience?

'I ... I ... suppose Tony wasn't able to race,' she managed to say.

His face hardened and he flashed her a hostile glance.

'Even now you are more concerned about him than you are about me,' he accused. '*Si*, he was able to race. He started late, but he soon caught up and was actually overtaking me when the accident happened. But he wasn't the one who sideswiped me.' His eyes narrowed unpleasantly as they focussed on something she couldn't see. 'I'm pretty sure it was Giuseppe Ganzetti who did that, in spite of what Mario said this morning. Three times he did it as we were going round a dangerous bend near the Ganzetti pits. It was the third swipe which sent my car spinning across the track in front of two oncoming cars. It was raining at the time and they skidded and crashed too.' He clutched his head suddenly with both hands. 'My God,' he muttered, 'I can feel the jolt which went through me then going through me now. Remembering is a painful business,' he added with an ironic twist to his lips as he looked at her. 'In more ways than one,' he added dryly.

'Have you any idea why Giuseppe Ganzetti would do that?' she whispered, horrified by what he had told her.

'I expect he hoped to slow me down, prevent me from finishing ahead of him. The Ganzetti Company were in trouble that year, their sales were falling off and they were desperate for a success in the Formula One races to boost their image. They would do anything to stop a Vitelli car from beating one of theirs. As you can see, they put me out of the running for good.'

'But you might have been killed, and that would have been murder!'

'No, it was an accident.'

'A deliberate one,' she argued. 'Can't you bring some sort of legal action against Giuseppe, now that you've remembered what happened?'

'So you believe me, and you weren't there,' he said softly. 'No, I couldn't bring a legal action. No witnesses. Only the Ganzetti family saw what happened and they are going to swear, apparently, that I imagined it. That I wasn't thinking what I was doing because something had upset me.'

'My letter,' she whispered, her hands going to her cheeks. 'Was it that?'

'I don't think so. I'd got that out of my system by punching Tony.' Cesare paused, then added slowly, 'You want a divorce so you can marry him?'

'No.'

'Then why?'

'I ... I ... er ... well, I told you in that letter. It seems the reasonable logical thing to do under the circumstances.'

'What circumstances?'

'Not living together and. ...'

'I have to remind you that the only reason we haven't been living togther for the past eighteen months is that you chose to run away and hide. If I could have found you I'd have made damned sure you'd have lived with me again.'

'How? By using cave-man tactics?' she challenged.

'I'd have used much more subtle methods than a cave man could ever dream of,' he replied. 'I have to tell you, Katryn,' he went on more coldly, 'that I don't believe in divorce and I am not going to divorce you. The fact that we married in haste does not make our marriage any less to my way of thinking.'

'Then . . . then I'll just have to divorce you, won't I?' she retorted shakily.

He went very pale and she heard his breath hiss as he drew it in sharply.

'You're going to find that very difficult,' he retorted.

'I don't think so. I'll think I'll be able to find sufficient grounds,' she replied coolly, her chin up, her eyes meeting his directly.

'You won't be able to do it in this country. Although some people, mostly in the upper classes, go in for divorce, it's still regarded by the majority of the population as barbarous, and ruinous, and so it is not accepted,' he argued.

'Then I'll have to see if I can arrange to divorce you in another country, won't I?' she countered.

'I'll fight you, Katryn, every step of the way,' he said between his teeth and she could tell by the ominous glitter in his eyes that his temper was rising. 'I'll fight you until you come crawling back asking for mercy.'

'You wouldn't be so cruel, so uncivilised,' she exclaimed.

'Try me and you'll soon find out,' he grated. 'I'm not going to let you destroy our marriage just because we haven't lived together for eighteen months.'

'I think it's time you understood that we don't have a marriage any more,' she retaliated furiously. 'It ended when I left you. And I wouldn't be here now if your family hadn't asked me. But I've done what they asked me to do. I've helped you to remember, so I'll be on my way. Goodbye, Cesare.'

She turned away and started off down the hill, trying to pretend that the trees and the rocks weren't blurring before her eyes which had filled suddenly with unwanted tears. She mustn't break down now, she warned herself. She must keep on going, keep her back turned to him.

'Katryn, where are you going now?' he demanded.

'Back to the house to do what you suggested,' she called back over her shoulders, and some little birds disturbed by the sound of her voice rose fluttering and whistling from the long grasses where they had been feeding and swooped away into the trees. 'I'm going to phone for a taxi to come and take me to Molino.'

'You won't get a bus to Milan now, it's too late.'

'Then I'll stay the night in the hotel as I should have done last night and I'll catch the bus in the morning. But don't worry about me, I'll be perfectly all right. I'm used to looking after myself. Goodbye.'

'Katryn....' Cesare broke off, then started to sweat. There was a thudding noise and the sound of grasses rustling. Kathryn whirled round. He was lying in an awkward position on the ground. His face the colour of putty, he tried to get up and failed. Closing his eyes and setting his mouth, he tried again, failed again and groaned.

Kathryn rushed towards him and flung herself down on her knees beside him.

'Oh, what is it? What have you done?' she exclaimed.

He opened his eyes to give her a hostile stare, then he rolled over and sat up.

'I think I've sprained my ankle,' he muttered.

'Left or right?' she asked, shifting along her knees towards his bare feet.

'Left. I think it must have happened when I slipped on a rock in the stream and it was that which made me fall and not cramp in the leg. Just now when I tried to follow you it turned under me again.'

She pushed back the still damp leg of his jeans. There

was a greenish-looking swelling between the ankle bone
and the instep.

'You could have done more than sprained it. You could
have broken a tiny bone,' she muttered, unable to look
away from the uncovered part of his leg. It was red and
blotchy, the marks of severe burning. 'You'd better put
your shoes on,' she added, and her voice sounded very
faint and far away as she struggled against the sickness
which was churning in her stomach at the thought of
him burning or being hurt in any way.

She brought his shoes to him, but didn't offer to help
him put them on. He couldn't lace up the left one over
the swelling, so he tied the laces together higher up the
shoes so that they wouldn't trail. Then he tried to get
up again and managed to stand on one leg.

'You're going to need help getting down the hill,' said
Kathryn. 'What a good thing you asked me to wait.'

'I hope you realise I haven't done this deliberately to
detain you,' he said in frostbitten tones. 'I'll manage to
get down the hill on my own. You go ahead and make
your phone call, since you're so keen to leave me again.'

'How can I leave you?' she retorted. 'You might fall
again and not be able to get up.'

His eyes glittered with pure hate and she felt a shiver
go through her, but she didn't back down.

'Stop being so stubborn,' she snapped. 'Put your arm
about my shoulders and lean on me, use me as a prop
while you hop on one foot. It's the only way. Unless
you'd like me to go and see if I can get help from one of
the other villas or a nearby farm for you? But you'd
have to promise me you'd stay here and not try to get
down the hill on your own.'

Eyes narrow, he stared at her and she could see the

struggle he was having with his pride in the tensing of his jaw muscles.

'You're so small and thin,' he protested. 'You can't help me.'

'But I'm quite strong really,' she insisted.

'You weren't strong enough to have the baby,' he went on in a low voice. 'I was very sorry when you fell down the stairs, Katryn, and you lost the child. I wanted to tell you when it happened, but you were unconscious for a long time and then too woozy with the anaesthetic they gave you at the hospital to notice anything I was saying to you. Then I had to leave to go to Holland. When I came back you were still far from well, and after-wards. . . .' He broke off, frowned and rubbed at his fore-head as if he were still having difficulty with his memory. From under the shadow of his hand he gave her a quick searching look. 'You don't believe me, do you?' he accused bitterly.

'I . . . I'd like to, but. . . .' Her turn to break off, to bite her lip and frown, avoiding his eyes. 'It's as if it hap-pened to two different people,' she whispered.

'It did,' he said dryly, and shrugged. He turned away from her to look down the hill. 'If we're going to go back to the house we'd better start off now. At my rate of pro-gress it's going to take hours.' He glanced at her over his shoulder. 'I'll be glad of your help,' he added curtly.

Moving forward, Kathryn put her arm about his waist. He lifted his left arm and put it round her shoulders.

'Tell me when you want to stop and rest,' he said.

'As long as you tell me when you want to stop and rest,' she retorted.

And together they began to go slowly down the hill.

CHAPTER SEVEN

THE sun slid behind a purple mountain peak. Rose-coloured light sparked with gold flushed the pale blue sky and violet shadows quivered across the sapphire lake. Long grasses and reeds tinted russet red rippled gently beneath the touch of the evening breeze and the boughs of the orange trees sighed softly as white blossom petals drifted away from them to fleck the ground beneath. Close by a bird whistled piercingly and repetitively, serenading its mate.

The idyllic evening scene filled Kathryn with vaguely romantic longings and she wished she could have lingered outside to watch the sun set. The walk down the hill had been very trying and she saw the glimmer of the pale pink walls of the Villa Rosa with a sense of great relief. She knew that all the way Cesare had been in pain. Something more than the sprained ankle was wrong with his leg. As a result of the pain he had been freezingly silent or searingly rude and had made no attempt to hide the fact he resented having to accept her help.

To avoid having to walk through thick undergrowth or scrambling over rocks and fallen trees they had had to zig-zag back and forth across the hillside. They had stopped many times to rest, but even so they had both become very tired. All she wanted now, she thought, was to flop in an armchair and drink tea.

She opened the back door and went into the kitchen

first to switch on the light so that Cesare could see his way in. He hopped across to the table and sat down abruptly on a chair, stretching his left leg stiffly before him. His brow was beaded with sweat which also stained his shirt in big dark patches. His face was ashen and there was a deep frown between his eyebrows.

'Do you have any pain-killers?' she asked.

'They're in a phial in my bedroom on the bedside table,' he replied.

Kathryn went upstairs, found the pills and returned to the kitchen. Cesare had eased his body forward on the chair so that his head was resting against the chair back and his eyes were closed, but the frown was still there.

'Cesare, perhaps you should go into Milan to see your doctor,' she suggested.

'What good would that do tonight? He'd only tell me to take those pills, drug myself into insensibility and go back to see him tomorrow,' he retorted without opening his eyes.

'Then to the hospital,' she persisted. 'You've got to do something. It isn't your ankle which is hurting....'

'Tomorrow,' he interrupted her. 'I have to go to the hospital for physiotherapy tomorrow anyway.' He rubbed a hand against his left hip and opened his eyes to look at her from under heavy lids. 'Give me the pills, *per favore*,' he said, holding out a hand. 'And some water too. They're the devil to swallow.'

'But you won't be able to drive with a swollen ankle,' she said, handing him the phial.

'I'll manage somehow,' he muttered, shaking two big pills from the phial into the palm of a hand. 'The water, Katryn, if you please,' he added coldly.

She went to the sink and unthinkingly turned on the tap. The pipe which brought the water into the kitchen banged noisily with an air-lock.

'You'll have to go and switch on the pump,' said Cesare practically. 'You'll find it in the basement just about under the place where the sink is in this room. The switch is on the wall. Leave both taps open for the water to come through. There'll be a lot of air in the pipes which will have to be forced out before the water will flow easily.'

She did as he told her and the pump started up at once. In the kitchen water gurgled in the taps, coming out in short spurts. She filled a glass with cold and took it to him. He tossed a pill into his mouth and swallowed it.

'Would you like something to eat?' she asked.

'If I don't have something I'm likely to pass out with hunger,' he returned dryly. 'Could you get me the crutches, please? They are in the study. I'll be able to move around with them.'

She found and fetched the crutches, placing them against the table near to his hand.

'I'll cook something,' she said.

'Not for me,' he replied coolly, balancing on one leg and fitting the crutches beneath his armpits. 'Bread and salami will do, and I'll get it for myself.'

He swung over to the refrigerator and took out a roll of pink salami sausage, then opened the cupboard where the bread was kept. By the time he was back at the table Kathryn had found a bread board and a knife.

'I'll cut the bread for you,' she offered.

'Stop fussing,' he snarled. 'I'm not going to cut myself if that's what you're worried about. Go and phone for your taxi. If one comes straight away for you you'll be in time for dinner at the hotel.'

'I ... I'm not going,' she said stiffly.

Half-way through cutting a thick slice off the long round Italian loaf Cesare paused and looked at her, his eyebrows rising in mocking surprise.

'No? But I thought you were very keen to leave now that you've done what you came to do,' he drawled, and then went on sawing through the loaf.

'I ... I'm not leaving you by yourself tonight,' she said in a rush, watching him slice the salami.

'Why not?' he asked, placing salami on the hunk of bread he had cut and biting into both.

'You're in pain, you can't walk properly and you might need help. And ... and tomorrow you might not be able to drive the car. I'm staying so I can drive you into Milan tomorrow.'

He sat on the edge of the table and studied her as he chewed.

'What makes you think I'll let you drive my car?' he retorted.

'Your common sense,' she countered sharply. 'If you have any.'

'You must, of course, please yourself,' he replied with a shrug. 'You can stay or leave, whichever, but if you stay we'll decide tomorrow who drives. All right?'

'All right,' she agreed. What else could she say in the face of such stubborn independence and dislike of a helping hand? Going across to the refrigerator, she searched for something to cook for herself. She supposed she could have managed too with a salami sandwich, but judging by the way Cesare was hacking at the crusty loaf and spicy sausage there wasn't going to be any left for her.

After some consideration she decided to cook some macaroni to eat with a cheese sauce. Ignoring Cesare, she went about the kitchen collecting the necessary ingredients and pans, humming to herself to keep her mind off him. When the sauce was cooked and the macaroni was simmering she took cutlery out of a drawer and turned to the table to set a place and to ask him if he would like to share the meal with her.

He wasn't there, yet she hadn't heard him leave the room. Only a few fluffy white crumbs on the bread board were evidence that he had been here. Setting the knives and forks down on the table, she darted impulsively to the door which led into the hall. There she pulled up short. Light streamed out from the study doorway. Cesare must be in there. No point in going to ask him if he was all right or if he needed anything—she would only be treated to a hostile glare and some sarcastic remark.

She tried to pretend she enjoyed eating alone, but again the quietness of the house, situated as it was in quiet countryside, oppressed her. This villa had probably known a lot of noise, she thought; the noise of volatile, happy Vitellis all talking at once, arguing and laughing, fighting and loving. It had known the noise of many children and by now would have known the noise of Cesare's children if he had married one of his own kind, a beautiful vivacious sparkling-eyed Italian woman like Sophia Barzini, instead of herself.

Why had he married her? *You and the night and the moonlight went to my head, I suppose*, he had said. *Spring fever*, Tony had suggested, at Monza. But Cesare had expected to stay married to her. He didn't believe in divorce, and she would have to do the divorcing just as she had done the walking out.

But how and where? It had all seemed so easy when she had written to Cesare and had suggested he divorce her. She had assumed he would jump at the chance to be free of her so her could marry Sophia. Never once had she suspected he could be so inflexible.

It would probably cost her a lot of money finding a way to divorce him and she would be paying lawyers for years. But what alternative did she have? Live apart from him yet always be tied to him legally? She had been doing that for eighteen months and hadn't found it to be the most comfortable of situations. Always at the back of her mind there were doubts about her own behaviour and always there were those terrible nights when she ached to be with him, enfolded in his arms, making love with him.

But then could she live with him again and pretend there was no other woman in his life? Could she be with him knowing Sophia was still there, a dark shadow waiting in the wings of the stage like an actress waiting for her cue to enter and play her part? She shook her head slowly from side to side as she took off the apron she had been wearing and hung it up. She knew herself too well to be only the second best woman in his life. She was too possessive, too much in love with him not to be first with him, always.

Being liberated meant simply having freedom to choose and she had always had that freedom. But if she didn't like either of the choices offered what was she supposed to do? Admit that she had hoped there would have been a third choice? That she had hoped Cesare would have told her he loved her and wanted her back, in the same way she had hoped when she had sent that letter to him that he would have dropped everything he was doing and come running to her to swear his undying love and beg her to begin their marriage all over again.

She made an impatient exclamation, irritated by her own romantic imaginings. Might as well wish for the moon as wish that Cesare behave like one of the romantic heroes in a book by Constance Dale.

Perhaps she should try talking to him again about what he could remember. His apology about the loss of the baby had shaken her a little and looking back she found she couldn't remember too much about that time either, only the terrible aching sense of loss and the feeling that in losing the child she had lost any love Cesare might have had for her.

She went along to the study. The light was still on, but he wasn't there. He must have gone upstairs, and she wondered anxiously how he had managed to negotiate them on crutches. She went upstairs too. Light slanted out from his bedroom. She tapped on the partly open door. There was no answer, so she looked into the room. He was in bed and seemed to be asleep, lying with his back to her.

Suppressing her disappointment because there would be no talk tonight, no chance to recall the past and perhaps unravel some of the tangle, Kathryn tiptoed across the room and switched off the light. Leaving the room, she went downstairs.

At ten-thirty she gave up trying to be interested in a film on TV. The walk up and down the hill, the emotional upheaval of the day had made her very tired, so she might as well go to bed too and hope to fall asleep.

She took her suitcase upstairs, unpacked her night-gown and the suit and blouse she intended to wear for travelling the next day. She visited the bathroom, put on her nightgown and was just turning back the bed-clothes when she heard the phone ring in the study.

Not bothering with her dressing gown as she wanted to reach the phone before it stopped ringing in case it was Emilia or Vincente phoning to enquire about Cesare, she rushed down the stairs. When she spoke into the receiver an attractive contralto voice answered her.

'Is that Signora Kathryn Vitelli?'

'*Si*, speaking.'

'Kathryn, this is Sophia Barzini. Do you remember me?'

How could she ever forget that smoothly contoured face, those large melting brown eyes, that elegant long-legged figure?

'I remember. How are you?' she asked, remembering to be polite.

'*Bene, grazie*. How are you?'

'Very well.'

'And how is Cesare?'

'He is very tired and has gone to bed. He's asleep,' replied Kathryn shortly. She was determined to convey to Sophia that she wasn't going to waken Cesare just to speak to her. 'May I give him a message?' she added.

'*Si*, I would like that. It seems he called on me last night. Please tell him I was so sorry I wasn't at home. I would like to have seen him. And ask him to get in touch with me next time he is in Milan, please. There is

so much he and I have to talk about. You are staying at
the Villa Rosa long, Kathryn?'

'I . . . er . . . I'm not sure. Is that all, Signora Barzini?'

'I wish you would call me Sophia. I feel we could be
such good friends, you and I. We have so much in
common.'

'Such as?' queried Kathryn stiffly. The gall of the
woman!

'Cesare,' breathed Sophia into the mouthpiece her end
of the line and then chuckled softly. '*Arrivederci*,
Kathryn.'

There was a click and the line went dead. Kathryn
replaced the receiver and stood for a moment seething
with jealousy, the nerves in her stomach twingeing and
twisting with the corroding, destructive emotion. This
was how it would be if she decided to stay and live with
Cesare, she thought, as she went slowly up the stairs.
She would have to put up with that woman phoning
him and dropping hints about her close relationship with
him, and it was something she couldn't tolerate.

She reached the landing and noticed the light was on
again in Cesare's room. Approaching the door as if
drawn by a magnet, she looked into the room, ruefully
admitting to herself that she couldn't stay away from
him. Even if they argued all night she had to talk to
him again, be near him in some way.

'Are you all right?' she asked tentatively. 'Can I get
anything for you? A drink?'

He was still lying with his back to the door and he
didn't turn to look at her.

'I thought I heard the phone ring. Did you answer it?'
he asked, and his voice sounded slightly slurred.

'Yes.'

'Who phoned?'

'Sophia Barzini.'

Kathryn advanced slowly into the room and stood at the end of the bed. Above the stark whiteness of the sheet which covered the lower part of his body the bare skin of his heavy shoulders had a faintly dusky sheen and beneath the thick glossy curls which coiled on the nape of his neck the silver chain glinted, seeming strangely delicate in contrast to the powerful muscles of his shoulders and neck.

Taking advantage of the fact that his eyes were closed, Kathryn let her eyes feast on the chiselling of his profile; the strong straight line of brow being carried on by the dominant nose; the curving sensual fullness of the perfectly shaped lips; the rounded jut of the chin. It was like the profiles she had seen carved in bas-relief on ancient Etruscan vases in the museum in Milan; handsome and remote yet tantalisingly familiar.

'What did Sophia want?' he asked, drawling the words out as if he were having difficulty in speaking

'She said to tell you she was sorry she wasn't at home last night when you called to see her and asked you to get in touch with her when you're in Milan next,' she replied woodenly.

He opened his eyes and turned his head slightly to give her a wary sidelong glance from beneath long drooping lashes. Then he heaved over on to his back and shifted up slightly in the bed so that his shoulders were propped by the plump lace-edged pillows. One eyebrow slanted upwards in mockery and his cheeks creased attractively as he grinned at her.

'You see, I told you I didn't stay half the night with her,' he taunted.

'But you have in the past,' she countered defensively.

'Ha!' He laughed, rather strangely, she thought. 'What do you know about my past? It was a long time ago before Sophia married Leo, before I married you, that I stayed a night with her. A long time ago,' he drawled sleepily, his eyelids drooping heavily.

'That isn't what I've heard,' she argued.

'What have you heard, and from whom?' he demanded. 'Tell me, my sweet and lovely innocent wife, what awful things you have heard about Sophia and me.'

'Cesare ... what is the matter with you?' she demanded, moving round to the side of the bed so she could see him better. Making a great effort, he lifted heavy eyelids and smiled at her.

'I'm high on the pills I've taken,' he murmured. His eyes narrowed and lunging across the bed he grabbed hold of her hand, pulled and, caught off balance, she fell on to the bed. Pushing her back against the pillows, Cesare leaned over her, trapping her with one arm bent across her chest, and studied her face with lazy mocking eyes.

'What have you heard and from whom about Sophia and me?' he asked again, his voice soft with menace and still slightly slurred.

'Tony told me at Monza that you and Sophia had been together a lot and....'

'And of course you believed him, your honest upright Englishman, you believed him,' he sneered.

'It wasn't only Tony,' she protested, trying to push his arm off and failing. 'Cesare, please let me go. I'm in a most uncomfortable position like this....'

'I'll let you go when you've answered my question,'

he drawled, and his eyes glinted with devilry. 'And maybe I won't.'

'When I saw Sophia at Monza she herself told me how much she admired you and how closely she had been following your racing career since she had returned to Italy,' she replied, and tried to move away again, because the weight of his arm, the casual drift of his fingers against the edge of the bodice of her nightgown, the way he was looking at her with that suggestive glint in his eyes were making her mind swing dizzily.

'Following my racing career closely does not mean that she slept with me after every race,' he said dryly.

'But it meant you and she had plenty of opportunity to renew your love affair and I know ... everyone had made sure that I knew ... that you and she had once been in love and had wanted to marry,' she whispered.

The silence in the room was so complete she could hear the beating of their hearts, hers swift and irregular, his slower and more steady.

'So, I remember now,' he said, and rolled away from her to lie propped against the pillows again. 'You were jealous and gave me hell every time I returned from a race meeting that summer. *Si*, I remember.' He spoke between set teeth and gave her a scorching glance of hate. 'I don't want to go through that form of hell again. Better to live in a haze of half-forgotten dreams than to remember that reality,' he added tautly.

'I had every right to be jealous,' Kathryn defended herself as she sat up.

'I don't agree. Sophia didn't go to those races just to watch me. She went to be with Mario. He was her lover at the time.'

'But they ... they're cousins,' she gasped.

'So what?' he jeered. 'Several times removed, and neither of them very moral. The Ganzettis have always been a bit freaky. But what's the use of telling you anything? You're not going to believe me. You prefer to believe Tony. You prefer to listen to trivial gossip about me and Sophia rather than believe me. I'm only your husband, so you mustn't believe me or trust me. You never have. What good is that?'

'But you and Sophia were going to be married once,' she argued. 'Cecilia told me that.'

'There's a certain amount of truth in that,' he admitted.

'And her parents didn't approve of you, so they stopped the marriage,' she persisted.

'That was the story Sophia put about when I changed my mind,' he replied dryly, and laughed a little self-mockingly. 'I was young and very idealistic when I fell in love with Sophia and it came as a shock to me to find out she had had several lovers before me. I had always hoped that the woman I married would be innocent. Sophia wasn't, so I didn't marry her.' Again his eyelids drooped sleepily. He stifled a yawn with the back of his hand and stretched lazily, his body and limbs moving with sensual grace beneath the thin close-clinging sheet. 'You know why I married you, Katryn?' he murmured, his words slurring into one another. 'Because you were innocent, as fresh and dainty as an unpicked rosebud.'

'Was that the only reason you married me?'

'Does there have to be any other reason?' he countered. His eyes were closed again, but his mouth was curling into a smile as if he liked what he could see behind the dark lids. 'The time had come for me to marry and start a family. You seemed to be a suitable woman to be the mother of my sons.'

'How cold-blooded! How calculating!' she seethed. 'How. . . .'

'Unromantic?' he challenged, opening his eyes suddenly and giving her another sardonic glance. 'Was your attitude any different?'

'What do you mean?' she countered uneasily.

'You wanted to show your cousin Jane you could grab a husband for yourself as well as she could, didn't you? One who was even better known and more wealthy than the one she had grabbed,' he jeered. 'And now like her you want a divorce, because marriage has turned out to be different from what you expected. You want to shrug me off as if I were an old gown you've grown tired of wearing because it's damaged and not as attractive as it once was.'

'That isn't so,' she protested. 'You got it all wrong. My wanting a divorce has nothing to do with you being crippled.' He had slid down and turned on to his side away from her. 'Oh, why won't you listen to me?' she cried angrily.

'I'm sleepy and I've had enough of reality for one day,' he muttered. 'I want to forget. Be good enough to close the door when you go out, and then if you should shout out in nightmare you won't disturb me like you did last night.'

She quivered all through the length of her body.

'So I didn't dream you were in bed with me last night,' she whispered, staring at his broad back. When he had turned over the sheet had slipped down below his waist and she could see the skin about his waist was as badly blotched as the leg she had seen that afternoon.

'No, you didn't dream that part. I was there trying to comfort you. It was pleasant, wasn't it? And I had hoped to make it even more pleasurable for both of us, but you went to sleep. But even just sleeping with you was good, Katryn, you're soft and supple to hold and you smell fragrant and you don't snore....' His voice slurred away into silence.

'Why did you come to me?' she asked, her voice shaking a little.

'What else is a husband supposed to do when his wife cries out in the night?' He let out a weary sigh. 'But I don't expect you to understand. You never have understood what marriage is all about.'

His bitterness rasped on her nerves. Her hands clenched on her knees, but she didn't move because her glance was held by those betraying marks on his back where he had been burned.

'I know you hate me, Cesare, because I don't understand what marriage is about, because I can't turn a blind eye and a deaf ear when you prefer the company of other women to my company,' she said in a low shaky voice. 'That's why I had to leave you and why I want a divorce. I couldn't and can't live with you knowing you still love Sophia and still go to visit her. I can't. I can't!'

Her voice broke. Something burst inside her, a warm deep emotion bursting through the restraint she had imposed upon it for so long. Her hands reached out and she laid them gently on the marks on his back and felt him stiffen.

'Go away, Katryn.' His voice was gruff. 'Go away.'

'I had no idea. I didn't know how badly you'd been burned,' she whispered, still touching him, stroking his back soothingly as if by doing so she could smooth the marks away.

'I told you I could have gone up in flames. Aren't you sorry I didn't?' he jeered. 'If I had you would have been saved all the trouble of looking for a way to divorce me.'

'That's a hateful thing to say,' she gasped. 'And you wouldn't say it if you weren't half stoned with those pain-killing pills. How many did you take?'

'I've forgotten,' he replied. 'I don't want to remember anything. I don't want to remember you or Tony or the crash. Go away, Katryn.'

Suddenly she was crying, tears sliding down her face. She tried to wipe them away with her hands, but they wouldn't stop. Sobs shook her and she sniffed. Cesare heard and turned his head to look at her in surprise.

'Why are you crying?' he demanded. 'I've never seen you cry before.'

'It . . . it's your back,' she muttered.

'Ah, yes, my burns,' he mocked. He sat up so that the sheet fell away from his body completely. There were blotches on his ribs reaching right down over his stomach and there were some shiny white patches where skin had been grafted on. 'Take a good look,' he taunted. 'There are more lower down on my thighs and legs. Would you like to see?' His hand began to lift the sheet from the lower part of his body. 'You'd be the only one to see them besides the doctors and the nurses.' His hand became still. 'But no, on second thoughts it would be best if you didn't see. They might shock you too much and make you cry more as you realised you're married to such a damaged specimen. . . .'

'Stop it!' she cried. 'Oh, stop tormenting me! I'm not crying because I'm married to you. I'm crying because you were hurt so badly. It's as if ... as if ... it had happened to myself,' she whispered. She wiped the tears from her face and began to slide off the bed. 'All right, I'll go and let you sleep. I know *you* don't need *me* to comfort you. Drugs can do that for you.'

Her voice broke again and she buried her face in her hands as another storm of weeping shook her. Never had she cried like this, not since she had been a girl and had been told her mother had died.

Cesare muttered something and shifted in the bed again. Putting his arms about her, he pulled her down on the bed beside him. He dragged the bedcovers from beneath her, gathered her against his warm bare torso and covered her. Then he cradled her, pressing her head into his shoulder as he had the night before, stroking her hair and her back soothingly, and gradually her tears dried up.

'There are times when I do hate you, Katryn,' he confessed softly against her hair. 'I used to hate you when we were first married.'

'Why?' she mumbled in astonishment, her lips moving against the warm skin of his shoulder.

'Because I felt you were using me as a substitute for Tony when we made love. You used to close your eyes when I kissed you as if you didn't want to see it was me kissing you; as if you were trying to pretend it was him. I think it used to make me go a little crazy and I was rough with you wanting to make you see *me*, feel *me*.' He laughed self-mockingly. 'I'm only a man, a human being like you with feelings that can be hurt, not a cold-blooded devil or a plaster saint.'

'I didn't know you knew how I'd once been in love with Tony,' she murmured. Now she was close to him she could feel the heat of him burning against her, through the thinness of her nightgown, and smell the musky fragrance of his skin. 'I thought it didn't show,' she excused herself. 'But after we'd been married a few months it was you I saw and felt, Cesare, I ... I wouldn't have wanted to have your child if it hadn't been that way.'

'You were so cold and indifferent after you'd lost the baby I thought you were blaming me for all you had suffered since you had conceived,' he whispered.

'I didn't blame you, I didn't,' she protested.

'Then why did you refuse to let me sleep with you?' he asked tautly. 'Why?' His fingers closed about the soft flesh of her upper arm and gripped bruisingly.

'It was you who moved out of our room into the spare room,' she argued, her glance going against her will to his mouth, inches above hers, the chiselled lips slightly parted, and the urge to press her lips to his and to seek their fiery urgent sweetness sprang up in the pit of her stomach and became an insistent ache.

'I moved out because every time I went near you, you repulsed me in some way. Sometimes you would nag at me with cruel words. Sometimes you would push me away as if my touch revolted you.'

'It was because I thought you'd been with Sophia or some other woman,' she defended herself.

'And you did it again this afternoon on the hill. There is no better way of showing a man you don't want him,' he said slowly, and his bitterness stung her.

His hand relaxed on her arm and slid upwards over the curve of her shoulder. He slipped fingers under the thin strap of her nightgown and started to slide it down over her arm.

'I thought you didn't want me any more because I'd lost the baby,' she confessed in a whisper. 'I knew the child was important to you. Your mother had told me that having a child would ... would cement our relationship.' She drew a deep breath which was shaky with the aftermath of her sobs. 'I'd tried so hard, Cesare, and then I felt I'd failed you. You went away so often and left me by myself, and then when you returned you seemed to take it for granted you could make love to me because we were married and for no other reason. It wasn't enough and ... and I felt the same way this afternoon.'

His hand moved away from her breast from which he had been slowly and expertly stroking away the bodice of her nightgown, and he shifted away from her a little.

'If that's how you feel you'd better get out of this bed now and go to the other room,' he hissed urgently, 'because when we're close like this in bed I can't help but take it for granted I can make love to you. Go on, get out. Go away. Comforting time is over for tonight. You've had all you're getting from me.'

His sudden rejection of her had the effect of coiling her emotions into a solid knot of frustration. She wanted to hit out at him, bang at his chest with her fists, pull his hair until it hurt him. Instead she lay there frozen into immobility, reminding herself that he wasn't quite sober because of the number of pain-killers he had taken and possibly didn't really know what he was doing or saying.

'Not making much effort to go, are you?' he taunted, and came close to her again, sliding a hand round to the small of her back and pressing hard until her hips were moulded closely against his and she was quiveringly and achingly aware of his powerful masculinity. 'If you don't go soon I'll begin to think you don't want to go. Come on, my little lioness, snarl, show your claws, fight for your freedom.'

She did move then, arching away from him, trying to break his hold, but the movement only brought her legs and the lower part of her body into contact with his while it gave him the opportunity to survey her throat and breast which was now half bared to the wanton, glinting, half-veiled glance of his dark eyes.

'Let me go, Cesare!' she seethed, but he only laughed and bending his head touched his lips to the base of her throat and moved his hand up to her breast, long fingers probing and pinching.

Gasping, she thrust her fingers into his hair and pulled at it until he cried out and raised his head. Faces close, they glared at each other, their eyes dark and glazed with rising passion, their breaths escaping from their slightly parted lips to mingle and heat the small space which separated them.

'Admit you don't want to go,' he taunted in a whisper. 'Admit you have the same fever that I have and it's leaping along your veins like fire, making you thirst for satisfaction. There's only one way to relieve such a thirst, *carissima*. Let's take that way, let's do it, then there'll be no more nightmares, no more hate, no more restless regret.'

'But. . . .' she began to protest, and got no further because his lips silenced her. Fighting for breath beneath the demand of that ruthless kiss, she was pushed over and back against the pillows. The weight of his body prevented her from moving, but she didn't want to move because his lips were trailing devastatingly across the tender skin of her throat and breasts so that sensuous delight was seeping through her body and down through her limbs. Her arms went about his neck and with a sound that was half a groan and half a sigh his body relaxed against hers.

'I hate you, Katryn,' he whispered against her lips. 'I hate you because you've tormented me in dreams for weeks with your soft white skin, your silky silvery hair, your flashing golden eyes. But this isn't a dream, is it? This is reality, and I have a chance to exorcise that hate, and I'm going to take that chance ... now.'

His lips claimed hers again and the fever burned through her blood. Her mind spun dizzily and she went whirling down into the vortex of voluptuousness where there was no hate, no pain and no regret, only the wild joyous ecstasy, the culmination of passion.

CHAPTER EIGHT

THE rising sun filled the bedroom with a tangerine glow and under the eaves the swallows swooped and twittered, busy with their building of nests. Kathryn came awake slowly, aware of a pleasant lassitude in her limbs. Sighing with contentment, she rolled over on the bed, expecting to find a broad bare back against which she could snuggle and finding only emptiness.

Cautiously she opened her eyes. Through her lashes she could see Cesare. He was sitting on the edge of the bed and he was fastening the buckle of his belt, having somehow managed to pull on his jeans. In the sunlight the skin of his bare shoulders had a golden sheen and as he reached out for the crutches which were propped against the bed, muscles rippled beneath the skin, like waves rippling beneath the smooth surface of a sun-gilded sea. Standing up, he fitted the crutches beneath his armpits and swung over to the chest of drawers. He opened a drawer, took out a shirt, pulled it on over his head and with one hand tucked the tails into his waistband. Then he swung towards the door.

Kathryn sat up in bed. The sheet fell away from her, revealing her slender, round-breasted figure.

'Where are you going?' she asked.

Half way through the door he turned to look back at her. His face was like one of those carvings again, dark and handsome, tantalisingly familiar yet superciliously aloof.

'To shave,' he replied coolly. 'Any objections?'

'No, of course not.'

'Good, then I'll be on my way.' He turned to go through the door.

'Cesare.'

'*Si?*' He paused in the doorway again but didn't look back.

'How ... how is your ankle this morning?' she asked in a rush. She had really wanted to ask him how he felt regarding her; whether his hate for her had been exorcised.

'The same. Swollen.'

'And your leg and hip?'

'The same. Nothing has changed. *Mi scusi.*'

He went through the door, the rubber tips of the crutches squeaking a little on the vinyl tiles which covered the landing floor. The bathroom door opened and closed quietly.

Hunching the sheet about her again, Kathryn lay down, memories of what had happened in that bed during the night crowding into her mind. *Nothing had changed.* Cesare's remark clanged in her mind like a fire-alarm. He had taken what he had wanted from her, found a temporary release from torment in her arms, but she mustn't assume that his feelings about her had changed. Was that what he meant?

She rolled her head from side to side and groaned. How could she have behaved with such abandonment, giving way to her own sensual desires so weakly, allowing him to do what he liked with her? And she had believed herself to be so strong, able to withstand any attempt on his part to stimulate her senses to such a pitch that she would plead for satisfaction. She groaned again. That was what had happened last night. She had been no better than he had.

No worse either. The thought was comforting. It had been a natural happening, something which should happen between a woman and her husband. But not when one of the partners was considering a divorce. Supposing she conceived? *Oh, God,* that was very likely, because neither of them had bothered with any precautions. Cesare had been too stoned on pain-killing pills to spare a thought for anything like that. And she hadn't used anything since she had left him—there had been no need. She hadn't wanted to sleep with any other man.

'Katryn?' His voice made her jump and she looked round. He was standing in the doorway looking at her. 'I'd like to be at the hospital by nine-thirty. That means leaving here about seven-thirty. It is now ten to seven. If you still want to go to Milan I suggest you get up and dressed and have something to eat.'

'Do you want me to go with you? Do you want me to drive?' she asked.

'If you want to go you can drive,' he said with a shrug. 'If you don't want to go I'll drive myself. I'm going to make some coffee now.'

He swung away through the door and closed it after him, and Kathryn stared at the panels frowningly. If she wanted to go, he had said. Of course she wanted to go with him. She couldn't let him drive with a swollen ankle and a leg that was hurting. To do that would be selfish in the extreme. Driving him to the hospital was the least she could do for him.

Throwing off the sheet, she jumped out of bed, snatched up her nightdress from the floor and pulled it on. She left the room and went along to the front bedroom, collected her toilet bag and returned to the bath-room.

Within ten minutes she was dressed, looking slim and elegant in her straight brown skirt and striped brown and white blouse, with her hair coiled tidily on top of her head. Taking up her suit jacket, she slung it over her shoulders and was about to leave the room when she noticed her half-open suitcase. Should she take it to Milan or not?

She would ask Cesare, she decided, and leaving the room went downstairs. It would be a way of opening up the subject of whether he wanted her back to live with him again. If he did want her to live with him he must ask her; he must trample that mulish masculine pride of his in the dust and invite her back. If he didn't do that then she would leave him again, go back to Monte and work for Constance, and eventually, some time in the distant future, she would find a way to divorce him.

The kitchen was full of bright sunshine and the fragrance of freshly made espresso coffee. Cesare wasn't there, so she helped herself to coffee, noting from the dishes he had left on the table that he had already eaten and drunk. She found an orange and ate it, then cut a slice from the loaf of bread on the table. When she had fin-ished she collected up the dishes, washed them quickly and put them to drain. It was seven twenty-five.

In the hallway she could hear the sound of Cesare's voice coming from the study, speaking quietly. She stepped into the room and waited by the door. He was talking into the phone and smiling as he did so.

'You are most kind,' she heard him say. 'Si, I promise. I will see you later after I have been to the hospital. Pardon? What did you say?'

From where she stood Kathryn could hear the sound of the voice speaking at the other end. It was a woman speaking and the cadence of the voice was familiar.

'*Non importa*. Never mind,' Cesare said, and the voice at the other end as the person who was speaking obviously became enraged.

'*Stia quieto*,' Cesare ordered peremptorily. 'I will see you later. *Arrivederci*, Sophia.'

He clanged the receiver down and pushed to his feet. Kathryn lingered for a moment at the doorway and they exchanged stares. He didn't say anything, but she was sure he knew that she had heard the last two words he had spoken.

She turned and walked out of the room. She had had her answer. *Nothing had changed* since she had last lived with him. Sophia was still there, like a dark shadow hovering over them. Sophia would always be there, so what was the use in staying?

She went upstairs, stuffed her nightdress and toilet bag in her case, snapped the locks closed and lugged it along the landing and down the stairs. Cesare was in the hall by the open door, leaning on his crutches waiting for her.

'So you have decided to go to Milan with me?' he said, his glance going to the case.

'Yes. You can't drive if your ankle is still swollen,' she said stiffly.

'I could, but it would be painful and I would find it hard braking,' he replied. 'And I daren't take any more of those pills,' he added with a laugh and a shrug. 'They make me as high as a kite so that I don't know what I'm doing—hardly the condition to be in when driving.'

He stared at her intently as if he expected her to make

some rejoinder. Or was he trying to make sure she got the message behind his remark? He hadn't known what he was doing last night when he had been high on the pain-killers, so what had happened between them didn't matter.

She decided not to reply and picked up her case again.

'Do you have to take that with you?' he asked.

'Yes, of course I do,' she replied as lightly as she could. 'Have you forgotten that too? I'm going back to Monte Carlo to my job. I've done what I came to do. I've helped you to remember.'

She went through the open door, and out into the colonnade. On the driveway in front the Vitelli car's red paint had a metallic sheen under the brilliant sun light and the vehicle had been turned round so that it was ready to be driven down the driveway to the road.

Kathryn walked to the back of the car and put the case down. It was another lovely morning and white mist was curling up in feathers from the shimmering flat surface of the lake. Above the mist the rocky shoulders of the mountains on the opposite shore glinted with reflected sunlight, twinkling violet, rose and gold. The air was soft, scented with orange blossom and pine resin.

Cesare closed the front door. The gravel on the path crunched under the rubber tips of the crutches as he swung towards her and the keys on his key ring tinkled. He fitted a key into the lock of the boot and raised the lid.

'Are you sure you want to take it?' he asked.

Bending down to lift the case, she glanced up at him. He looked as if he were in great pain. His face was pale and lined and his eye-sockets were very dark as if someone had painted them with black paint. She almost gave

in; almost said no, she didn't need to take the case because she was going to stay with him and look after him.
Then she remembered Sophia. Cesare didn't need her.
He had Sophia and he was going to see the woman later,
after he had been to the hospital.

'Yes, I want to take it,' she said coolly, and heaved the
case up and into the boot. The lid clanged down. Cesare
took the key out and handed the bunch of keys to her,
indicating which one was for the ignition. Then he
swung away to open the door of the car on the pas-
senger's side. He put the crutches in the back seat and
slid awkwardly, easing his left leg in stiffly, and she
could see him wincing with pain.

She took her place behind the steering wheel, fastened
the safety belt and put the key in the ignition. She ad-
justed the rear view mirrors to suit her and turned on
the engine. It started with a soft purring rumble. She
put it into gear and the car swept forward smoothly,
tyres crunching over gravel.

When she turned the car on to the road which zig-
zagged across the hillside to Molino the bright glare of
sunlight on its surface leapt up to dazzle her eyes. Cesare
opened the glove compartment and closed it again.

'Wear these,' he ordered quietly, and slanting a glance
sideways Kathryn saw he was offering her sun-glasses.
She took them gratefully and slid them on, and at once
everything became softer and more muted. She eased her
back against the comfortable support of the bucket seat
and settled down to enjoy driving the powerful machine
which had been entrusted to her.

Terraced vineyards and hayfields climbed the hill on
the left, green with new growth, and the stone walls and
slate roofs of old barns and farmhouses flashed by. Soon

Molino came into sight, a jumble of geranium red roofs which seemingly fell into the deeply blue lake. Small open fishing boats driven by outboard motors swerved across the flat shimmering water, their wakes sparkling with sunbeams.

Molino was bypassed. The road straightened out but still dipped up and down along the coast of the lake. In the distance under the brilliant yellow rays of the sun the waters looked brilliantly green about the silhouette of an ancient tower which soared up from a tiny island in the middle of the lake; Castello Minore, once the home and fortress of some aristocratic family and now a hotel.

Kathryn spared a glance from the road for Cesare. He had eased down in his seat and had closed his eyes. She was glad she was driving, she thought, because it required all her concentration. There was no time to think or worry about him or ponder on whether she had made the right decision.

Into the tunnel bored through a mountain she drove and out again. The road was curving downward now towards the plain. Ahead she could see the white strip of the Autostrada, the wide road which sweeps across northern Italy linking the east coast ports to the west coast, bypassing the cities but also giving access to them.

Soon she was driving along the service road to join the Autostrada, taking her place in one of the lanes of traffic which was surging towards the vicinity of Milan, that giant spider of a city which sits in the middle of its web of roads.

It was a busy time of the day as commuters hurtled along at high speed on their way to work, weaving in and out of lanes, chopping and changing to overtake

slower vehicles, beeping horns, shaking fists, jeering at
one another. Kathryn glanced again at Cesare. He had
opened his eyes and was watching the traffic.

'Where do I turn off?' she asked.

'At the exit for Sestos San Giovanni,' he replied. 'Move
out now and get over into the far right lane, otherwise
we'll be past the exit and on the way to Novarro. Now,
Katryn, go!'

Glancing in the mirror, she switched on the right in-
dicator and to the rhythm of its persistent click-click she
turned the steering wheel and drove into the next lane
behind a container lorry, then making sure all was clear
again moved into the far right lane. The lane diverged
from the others, became a service road and swooped
down to traffic lights at the junction with another wide
road coming down from Como.

'When the lights change, turn left and get into the
right lane again,' said Cesare. 'I want to call in at the
factory before going to the hospital to leave the drawings of the new engine for my father to look at.'

The traffic was heavy and slow-moving going into the
industrial suburbs of Milan. Factories loomed beside the
road and in the distance structures of concrete and glass
glittered in the polluted sunlit haze. A big sign showing
a red phoenix rising out of ashes appeared on the sloping roof of a long factory.

'Slow down and turn right into that entrance,' Cesare
ordered.

Carefully and low-speed, the long bonnet of the Vitelli
car nosed its way through the workers who were throng-
ing through the gateway to the big yard which surrounded the sprawling factory buildings. Once in the
yard Cesare directed Kathryn to drive towards a new-

looking building of white concrete and dazzling glass and to park in the space beside it which was marked by a placard bearing his name.

He reached over into the back seat for a roll of drawings he had put there.

'Would you mind taking them in for me?' he asked. 'It would save me having to bother with the crutches. Leave them at the information desk just inside those main doors and tell whoever is on duty there that they are for my father.'

'Is there any other message?'

'Just say I'll be in to see him after I get back from the hospital.'

Kathryn got out of the car and walked over to the steps which led up to the glass revolving doors. Inside she paused in the big hallway and looked round. The floor was an intricate mosaic of red, white and black tiles depicting the phoenix. In the centre was an example of the original Vitelli car, big and box-like with wire wheels and its gear-lever outside next to the brake lever. Bright red with softly gleaming brass fittings, it had been designed by Cesare's grandfather Romeo Vitelli, who had driven it in the first motor race ever to take place as long ago as 1895.

There was no one at the information desk, so Kathryn walked over to a board on the wall nearby which listed the names of the people using the offices in that building. Vincente's name sprang out at her. It seemed the President of the company had his suite of offices on the first floor.

She stepped into one of the elevators. The doors slid to softly and after pressing a button the lift whisked her up silently, coming to rest gently on the first floor. The doors slid open and she stepped out into a wide corridor carpeted in crimson and decorated with indoor plants in large Etruscan-type jars. Doors of the rooms off that wide corridor were all open and she could hear the chatter of people who had just arrived for work. A door with the word President painted on it was right at the end of the corridor. It was also open.

Kathryn knocked and listened. Two people were talking in the room and she recognised Vincente's voice. He broke off what he was saying and called,

'Come in.'

She stepped into the room. It was big, luxuriously furnished and had a wide picture window which overlooked the factory yard and had a view of the distant hazy mountains.

'Kathryn! What are you doing here?' Vincente came over to her. His grey hair was well brushed and his dark grey businessman's suit and crisp white shirt were a perfect fit. He looked suave and successful, but his eyes, so deep and dark like Cesare's, were anxious. 'Is something wrong? Cesare?' he spoke urgently. Then remembering the woman who was presumably his secretary and who was waiting quietly behind him, he turned and said, 'That will be all for now, Signorina Bianco.'

The woman nodded, gave Kathryn a curious glance and left the room, closing the door behind her.

'Cesare is outside in his car,' explained Kathryn. 'He asked me to leave these drawings for you. There was no one in the information desk in the hall, so I brought them up myself.'

'But why didn't Cesare bring them?' Vincente took the roll from her and laid it on his wide desk.

'He sprained his ankle yesterday when he went up the hill,' she explained.

'He went up the hill? *Dio mio*, what for?'

'To fix the water pipe.'

'Ah, I see. The pipe became blocked.'

'Yes. He's having to use the crutches again. I'm just going to drive him to the hospital. He has to go to the physiotherapy department today.'

'He let you drive him?' Vincente's eyebrows went up in mocking surprise. 'I wonder if you realise how honoured you are, Kathryn?'

'I think I do,' she replied with a slight smile. 'He says he'll see you when he returns from the hospital.'

He moved quickly to open the door for her.

'I'll come down with you to have a word with him,' he said, and they walked together along the corridor to the lift.

'So, Kathryn, how has it been going, out at the villa?' Vincente asked when they were in the privacy of the lift. 'Has he remembered any more?'

'He says he has remembered everything,' she said.

The lift came to a stop. The doors opened and they stepped out.

'Everything, eh?' commented Vincente. 'Then you have had an exciting time of it with him. But I am glad that you came, Kathryn, and I hope you don't regret coming.'

She didn't answer him but went before him through the revolving doors and down the steps to the car. He followed her, going to the side of the car where Cesare was sitting. Cesare let down his window. They greeted one another and talked fast, obviously about the drawings Kathryn had taken to Vincente.

She took her place behind the steering wheel again and waited.

'Kathryn tells me you have remembered everything,'

Vincente said, raising his voice a little now that they had finished talking about engines.

'I've remembered a lot that would have best been forgotten,' drawled Cesare dryly.

'That is not very flattering to your wife ... or to us,' Vincente rebuked him sternly. 'And the separation, is it over?'

There was a short strained silence while Vincente looked at each of them in turn and both of them avoided his severe dark glance.

'So?' he rapped. 'You have no answer? Either of you?'

'Katryn can answer,' said Cesare. 'It is something she has to decide.'

'Are you staying, Kathryn?' demanded Vincente.

'No,' she whispered, shaking her head, unable to look at him. 'Nothing has changed,' she added as if that would explain everything to him.

There was another strained silence. Then Vincente let out a noisy exasperated sigh and hit the side of the car with the flat of his hand.

'I am sorry,' he said. 'Emilia will be too. We hoped ... we hoped for too much, perhaps. Are you going back to Monte?'

'Yes. Luigi has the address.'

'Good, good. Then I will say *arrivederci*.'

'*Arrivederci*, Signor Vitelli. Please tell Signora Vitelli I'm sorry I wasn't able to do much housework for her.'

'*Si*, I will. I'll see you later, Cesare.'

He walked away and Kathryn turned on the ignition of the car.

'Will you tell me how to get to the hospital?' she asked stiffly.

'As soon as we get to the city,' Cesare replied. 'Go out now on to the road you came here on and turn right. It will take us about twenty minutes.'

The traffic had eased a little and the sunlight had grown brighter. The high skyscrapers of the city soared up, towers of coloured concrete and flashing glass. But it wasn't all modern and commercial, as Kathryn knew from the short time she had lived there. Turning a corner at Cesare's direction, she saw with a leap of delight at meeting an old friend the dazzling marble Gothic cathedral, the third largest church in the world, dominating the centre of the city, its lacy carved pinnacles seeming to pierce the blue sky with their twinkling points, its statue of the Golden Madonna shining like a beacon high above the piazza where people and pigeons wandered about.

Into the Piazza della Scala she drove, past the famous opera house and the glass-domed and glass-covered galleries of the shopping arcade known as the Gallery and then along a steep-sided canyon of office buildings, past high blocks of apartments where flags and washing fluttered, multi-coloured, from hundreds of tiny balconies to a brand new square building surrounded by a high wall which Cesare said was the hospital.

She drove up to the side entrance of the building which he said was the way into the physiotherapy department. He got out of the car and reached into the back seat for the crutches.

'Where shall I park the car?' she asked.

'Over there.' He jerked his head in the direction of a parking lot nearby. He fitted the crutches into place and swung away towards the entrance. Kathryn reversed the car, turned it and found a slot between a white Fiat and

a green Japanese car. The low rakish lines of the Vitelli
made the other two cars look like tin boxes on wheels.

Kathryn locked the doors of the car and then took
her case out of the boot. She looked across at the entrance. Cesare had disappeared. She would have to go
after him to give him the keys, so she left the case by
the car and walked over to the glass doors.

Inside the doors there was a pleasant waiting room
with a reception desk. Cesare was leaning against the
desk talking to the girl behind it, who was filling out a
form.

'I've brought you the car keys,' said Kathryn, stepping
in front of him when he swung on the crutches in the
direction of the coloured chairs in the waiting area
where some patients were already sitting waiting for
attention.

Cesare stopped, leaned on the crutches and looked
down at the keys in her hand, then looked up and
directly into her eyes.

'You're not going to wait for me?' he said, but there
was no surprise in his face or in his voice. It was more
of a statement of fact than a question.

'No. I ... I'll find a taxi to take me to the station. I
expect I can catch a train to Genoa and go from there
to Monte by bus,' she muttered. 'If you need someone to
drive you back to the factory I'm sure one of your
brothers would come out here ... or perhaps even
Sophia would oblige.'

He frowned and his dark eyes gleamed menacingly
at her, but he didn't say anything. She supposed the
place was too public for him to speak his mind. His
glance went to the keys she was offering and slowly he

raised a hand and took them from her. He pushed them into the back pocket of his jeans.

'Katryn,' he said, and then broke off to glance round as a woman in a white nylon uniform entered the waiting area from a corridor and exclaimed,

'Signor Vitelli, on crutches again? I thought you'd given them up. What have you been doing? Come on now, we're waiting for you. You're late this morning.'

'*Mi dispiace*—I am sorry. I was delayed.' Cesare was smiling that smile which would defeat most women and grasping hold of the crutches he began to swing towards the woman, who in spite of the severity of her words was smiling back at him pleasantly.

Then he stopped, turned back to look at Kathryn and returned to her.

'Thank you for coming,' he said politely, his face impassive as a statue's, his eyes as deep and dark as two empty wells. Bending his head, he kissed her briefly on the cheek. 'Take care how you go. *Arrivederci.*'

He turned away abruptly, said something to the waiting physiotherapist which made the woman laugh and went with her down the corridor.

For a moment Kathryn lingered, suppressing an urge to go after them and demand to know what was going to be done for the pain he was suffering in his left leg, make her presence felt as his wife who was concerned about his welfare. But Cesare wouldn't like that, she thought with a sigh. He didn't want her with him. With a few polite words he had gone from her, accepting without argument the fact that she was going to leave him again. The dark shadow of Sophia had come between them, to blight their spring meeting and to part them again, perhaps for ever.

She left the hospital, found a taxi and travelled to the station. She didn't remember too much about the journey back to Monte; she supposed she must have been too numb for her memory to record details. But she did remember the sun shone all the time out of a cloudless sky and was still shining when at last she reached L'Hermitage, high on its bluff of rock above the glittering city of Monte Carlo. Only four days had passed since she had left with Luigi and yet she felt as if she had lived four years in that time, she felt so tired and so old.

She put down her case in the wide entrance hall. From somewhere on her left came the unmistakable sound of a typewriter being tapped slowly. Kathryn's lips moved in her first smile that day and she walked in the direction of the room where Constance did her writing.

The door was slightly open, so she went straight in. The room was hazy with bluish-grey cigarette smoke and Constance was sitting behind the desk, peering forward through her bi-focals at what she had typed on the paper inserted in the typewriter.

'How's it going?' Kathryn asked, and the novelist jumped visibly, looked up in surprise and then sank back on her chair, her hand going to her ample bosom.

'My God, Kathryn, you gave me a fright!' she exclaimed. 'You move about as silently as a ghost!' She leaned forward and peered again, muttered something about her glasses and whipped them off, then looked at Kathryn without them. 'You look as white as a ghost too. Are you really here or am I imagining you?'

'I'm really here.'

'Why didn't you let me know you were coming?'

'I ... there wasn't much time. I ... just came. You

said I could come back here if ... if....' Kathryn's lips began to tremble suddenly and she couldn't go on.

'If it didn't work out,' Constance finished for her slowly, and rising to her feet came round the desk towards her. 'I gather that it didn't.'

Kathryn nodded, swallowed and said,

'Do you still need a secretary, and will you employ a woman who is separated from her husband?'

'I certainly do need a secretary. I can't type for toffee,' said Constance forcibly. 'And since I'm familiar with the quality of your work I'm willing to stretch a point and employ you.' She went a few steps closer to Kathryn and studied her closer. 'When did you last eat, love?' she asked in a motherly way.

'I ... I don't know. I can't remember,' Kathryn muttered. Now she was at journey's end she felt very faint.

'Then I think it's time you ate now,' replied Constance. 'And while we're dining you can tell me all about what's happened.' She sailed off towards the door. 'Daisy?' she called, going out into the hall. 'Daisy, love, where are you?' Daisy must have answered her because Constance went on as she went off down the hall, 'Kathryn is back, so I think we'll have dinner early. She's starving!'

CHAPTER NINE

KATHRYN dragged her thoughts back from what had happened in May and rose slowly to her feet. The feeling of morning sickness had passed and she felt more able to cope with the day's work. By now the mail should have been delivered. Almost against her will her steps quickened and she almost ran down the steps of the terrace and along the short wide driveway to the letter box at the gateway. There might be a letter for her today; a letter with an Italian stamp and postmark.

Only three letters lay in the letter box and they were all for Constance. Kathryn let the familiar ache of disappointment have its way with her and then began to walk slowly back to the house. All summer she had been expecting a letter, if not from Cesare then from his mother or Cecilia, his sister, or even from his father. She had been so sure one of them would have kept her informed about him.

She had been living in hope from day to day; living on her nerves, so that in spite of the comfort of the house she was living in, the good food, pleasant company and interesting work she had lost weight.

It was so unfair that living apart from Cesare should do this to her, she thought, suddenly angry with herself as she climbed the stairs to Constance's bedroom. She should be able to manage without him. He could manage without her and had made it very obvious that he could when she had stayed with him at the Villa Rosa.

She shouldn't have gone to see him, that had been a mistake. If she hadn't seen him again ... her teeth dug painfully into her lower lip and her hand went to her waistline, spreading over its slenderness as if in search of a change. Her mouth twisted ruefully. She was going to pay for that mistake she had made.

Constance was out of bed and was sitting in front of the triple mirrors of her ornate dressing table making up her face. In the middle mirror which reflected the shimmering pink and white bedroom she watched Kathryn approach her as she fixed false eyelashes in place. When Kathryn placed the letters on the dressing table she glanced sideways at them.

'Open them,' she ordered.

The first envelope contained a bill. The second one contained a letter from a certain charity asking for a donation. The third one contained a handwritten letter from someone who had signed himself: 'Your loving nephew, Sam.'

'Sam?' exclaimed Constance, clapping her hands together in delight. 'Read it to me. What does he have to say? He's my sister's only son, thirty-six and a bachelor. I've invited him many times, but he's always had something else to do. He goes bird-watching for his holidays —I mean real birds, you know, the sort with wings that fly, not girls.' Constance placed a wig of ash-blonde waves on her head, and shifted it about a little until it was in a position which was comfortable. 'He might like you, though, Kathryn,' she added, picking up a silver-backed hand mirror and regarding her face more closely. 'Do you think I've put too much rouge on?'

'Yes,' said Kathryn frankly, and began to read the letter to herself. 'He's arriving in Monte today,' she said.

'He says he'd like to stay a week before going on to Kenya where he's going to spend the rest of his holidays watching wild animals in their natural surroundings.'

'Today? What time? We'll have to meet him. And we'll have to take him about while he's here, introduce him to some of the night spots, take him to the Casino, if we can get him to part with some of his money.' Constance paused, her eyes narrowing as she stared at Kathryn. 'You don't look well this morning. Daisy tells me you've been off your food and have felt nauseous in the mornings. When you're in town today you can visit my doctor. I've made an appointment for you. It's at eleven o'clock.'

'Oh, but. . . .'

'You'll do as I ask,' Constance went on firmly. 'I can't have you being ill. Now off you go to do your shopping. And don't think for one minute you can dodge the visit to the doctor. I'll be checking up with him to make sure you've been to see him.'

Dr Côté was cool and efficient and after examining her and giving her various tests confirmed that she was probably eleven weeks pregnant. He advised her to eat more, prescribed iron pills because he thought she might be a little anaemic and recommended that she visited his pre-natal clinic every month.

In one way his diagnosis made her feel better. She was going to have Cesare's child again, and this time she was going to make sure it was born and survived. She was going to take care of herself.

But she would have to tell Cesare. He had a right to know, and there was a problem. She didn't want him to feel he had to have her back to live with him just because she was going to have his child or because he felt it was his duty as her husband and the child's father.

The problem of how to tell him and when to tell him niggled at her all day. Even the arrival of Sam Lowe didn't distract her from it. A tall, thin, brown-haired man with a shy smile and narrow light blue eyes, he seemed to be genuinely fond of Constance and teased her often but gently about her success as a novelist.

During the next few days Kathryn was often in his company because Constance was very keen for him to see as much of Monaco and the French Riviera as possible, and using her own age and her inability to get going in the morning as an excuse, encouraged Kathryn to take him about during the daytime.

Night-time was a different matter. Then Constance always came alive and every evening of Sam's stay all three of them drove down into Monte to dine at one of the many fine restaurants and afterwards visit the theatre, one of the casinos or a night-club.

Kathryn found Sam to be an intelligent and undemanding companion. He was a reluctant gambler, but seemed to find a great deal of pleasure in watching the people, many of them well-known celebrities from all over the world who could be seen in the old Casino or in Loew's American casino. He was an even more reluctant dancer, although he did make an effort to circle the floor with Kathryn at the night-club which they visited on his last night.

Constance had invited John Carey and other friends to join her for dinner and the visit to the night-club that night as a farewell party for Sam. But none of the men present were really dancers, thought Kathryn as her feet tapped in time to the rhythmic beat of loud music.

The night-club was the one in which she had first

danced with Cesare, and although the decor had been changed the atmosphere was the same, dim flickering lighting, tables crowded closely together, the glitter of jewels against sun-bronzed skin, the rumble of many voices, the tinkle of glasses and always the hypnotic beat of drums and electric guitars and the swaying and twisting of bodies in the darkness and the heat . . .

She couldn't stand it any more. She couldn't sit there longing to dance, above all longing to dance with Cesare. She had to get out before her mind burst. Rising to her feet, she excused herself, saying she was going to the women's room.

Hardly looking where she was going, she threaded her way through the tables and lifting the long skirt of her evening gown she went up the flight of shallow steps to the entrance foyer, sparing a brief glance only for the man who was just entering the club. Tall, shiny black hair, a dark red shirt and an elegant white suit; she dismissed him as one of the latin types Daisy Hardcastle didn't care for and went on her way towards the women's room.

When she returned to the foyer, she hesitated, wondering whether to leave and go for a walk or whether to go back to the party. She had made a couple of steps towards the door when a voice spoke behind her.

'Don't go yet. Stay and dance with me.'

Breath catching in her throat, she turned and looked up. Dark green eyes with a glint of amusement in their depths looked down the length of a Roman nose at her. Well-shaped lips slanted upwards in a smile.

'Cesare!' Her lips formed the name, but her voice was non-existent. Why hadn't she looked more closely at a man who wore a dark red shirt with a white suit? Why

hadn't she realised he was the man she had been longing for all evening? Her glance went to his legs. 'How
can you dance?' she whispered.

He laughed, spread his arms wide in a flamboyant
gesture.

'No stick. No crutches,' he boasted, and grabbed one of
her hands. 'Come on,' he urged, and began to pull her
towards the steps.

'Wait, wait. . . .' She hung back. 'You can't turn up
like this and expect me to dance with you without telling me why you're here.'

One tug on her arm and she was falling against him
and his arms were holding her closely.

'I have come here to see you,' he murmured into her
hair. 'It's taken me most of the evening to find you. The
housekeeper at the villa where you live was very vague.
"They're dining out, then going to a night-club," she
said. It's a good thing your employer is well known or
I might not have tracked you down so soon. Now, will
you dance with me, *per favore?*'

Kathryn had no alternative to offer and no desire to
refuse. Soon the rhythmic beat had taken over both of
them and they were swaying and twisting with the other
dancers, sometimes apart, sometimes close together, arms
about each other, betraying by every move they made
and every glance they gave each other their joy at this
meeting in the place where they had first met.

When the music ended Cesare took her hand and led
her off the floor.

'And now we go somewhere to talk,' he said auto-
cratically.

'I'll have to tell Constance,' she said. 'Come over here
to meet her.'

It wasn't necessary for her to introduce Cesare because John Carey had recognised him and was on his feet to shake him by the hand, delighted to meet at long last the driver he had admired so much. To Constance Cesare was persuasively polite and she had no hesitation in agreeing to his suggestion that he should take Kathryn for a drive along the coast.

'But don't keep her out too late. She hasn't been well lately,' she said.

'What's wrong?' Cesare's eyes were suddenly sharp as he looked at Kathryn.

'I'll tell you later,' she replied coolly.

Floodlights gilded the pale stone of the front of the Casino and the bronze angels supporting its clock and the green of its domed roof gleamed softly. The same light illuminated the fronds of the palm trees edging the square and shone on the smooth dark red paint of the Vitelli car. The shadows of the trees flicked over the car as it moved almost silently away from its parking place in the direction of the corniche road which swooped down to the coast.

On a sea ruched with waves the dazzle of moonlight shimmered. The sky was dark blue velvet pinpricked with the diamonds of stars and far away in the distance another light flicked on and off at regular intervals, a warning to whoever was sailing the sea.

It wasn't as far as Kathryn had remembered to the place where Cesare had stopped over three years ago, but the view was the same, breathtakingly romantic. the air coming through the windows was summer-warm, fragrant with the scents of plants and salt, loud with the songs of crickets and the whisper of waves.

'Why have you come?' she asked. 'Why do you want to see me?'

'To answer a letter you sent to me,' he replied.

She turned to look at him. He was sitting far away from her, leaning against the car door, and in the moonlight his face was a remote mask of silvered skin and deep shadows.

'I would have come to see you as soon as I received it, only I was involved in an accident and I've only just learned to walk properly again, without a limp,' he continued quietly, and added with a touch of bitterness, 'I had it all planned. After the race was over in Barcelona I was going to drive straight here to tell you I had no intention of divorcing you then or at any other time. I was going to tell you that I loved you and wanted to live with you always and for ever. I was going to take you back to Italy with me. My intentions went up in flames with your letter.'

She stared at his profile, bewildered by what he had just said. Had his memory been playing tricks again? Had he forgotten she had visited him in May? Did he believe that what had happened at the Villa Rosa was one of those half-forgotten dreams he had known when he had been recuperating?

'Cesare, have you forgotten that....' she began diffidently, and he leaned towards her suddenly.

'I have forgotten nothing,' he answered. 'I've remembered everything, but I told you I had in May.'

'Then perhaps you've remembered that you told me to leave you,' she replied, feeling relief wash through her. 'When were were in Monza,' she added.

'Si, I remember that. I said it in anger and I didn't really think you would take it seriously. I was tired and frustrated that morning because my car had broken down and you didn't seem to care. You kept on about Sophia.' He paused and sighed. 'I should have taken more time to be with you, I can see that now. I should have realised that there was something wrong, poisoning our relationship. I did realise ... after you'd gone. But then it was too late. I couldn't find you.' He took a deep breath and added in a taut low voice, 'Katryn, if you knew what I went through when I couldn't find out where you'd gone or where you were, believing you were with that blond-haired, blue-eyed, two-faced Tony. ...'

'You went through what I went through believing that you were with Sophia when I had to stay in Milan,' she said. 'You were jealous.'

'Si, I was jealous,' he said between his teeth. 'I was half crazed with jealousy, fighting mad with it. That's why I hit Tony.' Shifting his position, he slid an arm along the back of her seat and bent his head towards her. 'Katryn, I love you and I'd like you to live with me always. I wanted to ask you to stay with me in May and begin our marriage all over again, but I couldn't.'

'Why couldn't you?' she gasped, turning to him and finding that their lips were within kissing distance.

'Because I felt at a disadvantage with you.'

'Whatever do you mean?'

'I couldn't walk properly and I was mad with pain half the time. I couldn't ask you to give up your freedom and your new job to live with me because I was afraid you would agree out of a sense of duty or pity. I couldn't ask you until I was on equal terms with you again.'

'Pride, stupid, mulish masculine pride,' she hissed at him.

'Si, pride,' he retorted. 'And it isn't necessarily masculine. You're not going to tell me you have none, because I know differently. You think I didn't read between the lines of that letter you sent? You think I didn't understand that you were using the suggestion that I divorce you as an excuse to write to me so that I would know where you were? Weren't you expecting me to show up in Monte that spring to renew the promises we had made two years earlier?'

'Yes, I was,' she admitted, and he took hold of one of her hands and raised it to his lips to kiss each finger in turn.

'So here I am, *carissima*. Am I too late? Will you begin our marriage all over again?'

It was what she had wanted to hear, what she had longed to hear. Emotion swelled up in her, threatening to overcome her, but still she had reservations.

'Are you going to race again?' she asked coolly, removing her hand from his.

'Perhaps, but not to the exclusion of everything else,' he replied. 'Would you object?'

'Not as long as....' She broke off, then added in a hurried whisper, 'What about Sophia? Cesare, is she ... is she your mistress?'

'Good God, no, and never was. How often do I have to say it before you'll believe me?' he said fiercely.

'But you were going to see her the day I left you in May, I know you were because I heard you talking to her on the phone.'

'Eavesdropper,' he taunted. 'And your eyes should be green, my love, you're so jealous. If you had stayed in Milan that day you would have gone with me to see her. I went there at her suggestion because she wanted to tell me what she had seen at the race in Barcelona and she wanted to tell me in front of Mario.'

'What did she see?'

'What the other Ganzettis saw, only wouldn't admit to. She saw Giuseppe sideswipe me. She also heard him and Mario discussing the idea before that race.' He laughed dryly. 'Naturally Mario was furious with her for telling me.'

'Why did she tell you?'

'I don't know. Maybe because she still had a *tendresse* for me. Maybe because she was trying to get even with Mario for something he had done to her.' He shrugged. 'There was always a lot of infighting among the Ganzettis. As you can guess, Sophia and Mario are no longer lovers. In fact she'd gone to the States again and I believe she's going to be married to a Texas cattle baron whom she met when she lived over there before.' He moved closer to her again. 'If you'd stayed in May, you'd have known all about this,' he murmured.

'You could have written to tell me, or you could have come to see me,' she retorted. 'Luigi had my address.'

'I couldn't come until I'd found out if the operation was successful and I could walk without a limp,' he said.

'You had another operation?' she exclaimed.

'*Si*. I was admitted to the hospital the day after you left. It was your visit to me that spurred me on to have it.'

'Why wasn't I told?' she demanded, sitting up straight and turning on him. 'Why didn't one of your family write to me and tell me?'

'Because I told them not to.'

'Oh, now who's arrogant!' she fumed, thinking of how she had looked for a letter every day.

'I had to be sure it was a success,' he said urgently. 'I

wanted to be able to come to you un-crippled. Is that so hard to understand?'

'I understand,' she muttered. 'Oh, I understand. You have to be the strong one, the one in authority.' She shook her head from side to side, hugging her arms about her because she felt suddenly cold. Staring out at the moon-dazzle on the sea, she wondered how she was going to tell him she was pregnant. She was the one who was at a disadvantage now. 'It's late and it's cold. I'd like to go back to L'Hermitage, please,' she said weakly.

'Not yet. Not until you tell me whether our separation is over. Katryn, you're the only woman I've ever loved in this way, the only one I've ached to be with, the only one I've been jealous about. I want you because you're you, not just because you'll be a suitable mother for my children, but because you're independent and lively, because you make fun of me ... for many, many reasons I can't put into words.'

She turned suddenly and flung her arms about him, tilting back her head to look up at him.

'I love you too, Cesare, for many many reasons. I love you more than anyone else in the world and I wouldn't have left you that second time if I hadn't heard you talking to Sophia on the phone. I was going to stay with you and look after you and help you to learn to walk again, not because I was sorry for you or because I felt it was my duty as your wife, but because I love the stubborn, arrogant person who is you. I love you and I want to live with you always and for ever, anywhere.'

His hand pulled at the topknot of her hair and it fell about her cheeks. His mouth covered hers hungrily and his arms gathered her slenderness against his warmth.

The kiss was deep and long as each of them tried to convince the other of the sincerity of their feelings, and when it was over they were both breathless.

With one arm still about her Cesare started the car, reversed it with casual expertise and drove off in the direction of Monte.

'You'll have to tell me which way to go,' he said.

'Take the first road you come to. It's the last house,' she replied, nestling her head into the curve of his shoulder. 'Which hotel are you staying in?'

'I haven't booked in anywhere. I was hoping a certain young woman I know might find room for me in her bed,' he replied lightly. 'Do you think she will?'

'I know she will.'

'We have a lot of lost time to make up for,' he sighed.

'We can start doing that tonight,' she replied softly.

Lights were on in the villa, but all was quiet. They crept up the stairs hand in hand to Kathryn's room. She switched on the bedside lamps, closed the door and then turned down the bedcovers. Going across to Cesare, who was taking off his jacket, she made a deep curtsey.

'I hope the room is to your liking, *signore*,' she said.

'You're very comfortable here,' he replied, looking around the dainty white and green room with its frilled curtains, thick carpet and wide satin-covered bed. 'Perhaps you're too comfortable,' he added coldly, walking over to her and standing over her in a threatening way. 'So comfortable you don't want to leave and come back to Italy with me.'

'Don't tell me you're jealous of my job,' she taunted.

'I'm jealous of your job, of your Constance Dale, of all those people you were with tonight, of anything and anyone that takes you away from me,' he snarled softly, and sliding two fingers inside the low V of the bodice of her gown he pulled her towards him and kissed her with a savagery which sent desire shooting along her nerves like a shower of sparks from a firework. Swaying a little under that erotic onslaught, she wound her arms about his neck, her fingers tangled in his hair, and she went limp against him.

'Carry me, Cesare,' she whispered. 'Carry me to bed like you used to do.'

At once he lifted her in his arms and carried her over to the bed, his dark glance never leaving her face, thrilling her with its passionate possessive message.

On the bed they lay close together, kissing and fondling, stroking clothing away from each other. Kathryn cried a little because there were still marks where Cesare had been burnt and he sighed because she seemed to have lost weight. And then they were even closer together, as close as they could possibly be, and the cries and sighs were of joy because they had found each other again.

After the ecstasy of reunion Kathryn lay enclosed in the loving warmth of his arms, so contented that she feared to speak in case she destroyed the harmony between them. But she would have to tell him before she slept, before the dawn of a new day.

'Cesare.'

'Mmm?'

'Would you be jealous of another baby?'

The fingers which had been stroking her back in the lazy sensuous aftermath of loving were suddenly still. Then he moved roughly, his hands on her arms, pushing her away from him so that he could see her face. Dark yet bright, his eyes were puzzled.

'When?' he demanded.

'Nine months from the end of May.'

'*Dio mio*, you are sure?'

'The doctor confirmed it today.'

His eyes narrowed suspiciously and he lay on his back, away from her.

'If I hadn't come to see you today were you going to write and tell me about it? Or would you have come back to Italy to tell me?' he asked in a low voice.

'I don't know. I hadn't decided,' she muttered, pushing up an elbow so she could look down at him.

'Don't you want the baby, Katryn?' he said quietly.

'Oh, yes, very much, because it's yours.' She put a hand on his chest, her fingers spreading out in an urgent caress. 'You must believe that, Cesare, but I don't want you to think ... I mean I was unsure about telling you because ... Oh, please don't laugh. Listen to me!' she stormed, beating her fist against his chest as he began to shake.

'I am listening, my love.' His arms went round her and he pulled her down on top of him. 'But I can't help laughing at you because you make everything so complicated. Why should you be unsure about telling me about my own child? What is it you don't want me to think?'

'I don't want you to think I want to end our separation just because I'm going to have a baby, and I don't want you to think you have to have me back because you're its father,' she replied seriously.

The dark eyes glinted at her mockingly and the well-shaped mouth curved derisively.

'If you don't want me to think that, you'll have to use all your charm and all your feminine wiles to persuade me to think otherwise, won't you?' he scoffed. 'Why don't you do that now, *cara*? You'll find me very receptive and open to persuasion when you are doing the persuading. Let me show you how to begin.'

Their lips met again and as the sweet sensuous shivers tingled through her body again Kathryn knew that all the dark shadows which had hovered over their marriage were fading fast before the flames of their newly-kindled love. The past was already a dim, almost forgotten dream. The present was real, something she could see and feel, and the future blazed with brightness.

Titles available this month in the Mills & Boon ROMANCE Series

CHATEAU IN THE PALMS *by Anne Hampson*
Philippe de Chameral could have made Jane happy. — but
he did not know that she was a married woman . . .

SAVAGE POSSESSION *by Margaret Pargeter*
Melissa had been too used to having her own way to allow
Ryan Trevelyan to dominate her — but she soon had to
change her tune!

ONE MORE RIVER TO CROSS *by Essie Summers*
Rebecca was as different from her flighty cousin Becky as
chalk from cheese, but the girls' identical appearance was to
get Rebecca into a difficult situation with the bossy Darroch . . .

LURE OF EAGLES *by Anne Mather*
An unknown cousin had inherited the family business, and
Domine found herself agreeing to the masterful Luis Aguilar's
suggestion that she accompany him to South America to meet
the girl.

MIDNIGHT SUN'S MAGIC *by Betty Neels*
Could Annis ever make Jake see that she had married him for
love, and not on the rebound?

LOVE IS A FRENZY *by Charlotte Lamb*
Seventeen-year-old Nicky Hammond's devotion was touching,
but Rachel couldn't possibly return it. Yet how could she
convince his disapproving father Mark that she wasn't cradle-
snatching — or worse?

THIS SIDE OF PARADISE *by Kay Thorpe*
Gina's so-called friend was after a man with money, so Gina
couldn't really blame Ryan Barras when he got entirely the
wrong idea about her . . .

A LAND CALLED DESERET *by Janet Dailey*
LaRaine had always been able to twist men round her finger
but, as luck would have it, she fell in love with Travis
McCrea — who had no time for her at all!

TANGLED SHADOWS *by Flora Kidd*
Kathryn could hardly refuse to return to her husband when
she learned from his family that he had lost his memory in
an accident — but would he remember what had destroyed
the marriage in the first place?

THE PASSIONATE WINTER *by Carole Mortimer*
Piers Sinclair was her boy-friend's father: older, more
sophisticated, far more experienced than she was. And so of
course Leigh fell in love with him . . .

— all that's pleasurable in Romantic Reading!
Available October 1979

Forthcoming Mills & Boon Romances

THE KURRANULLA ROUND *by Dorothy Cork*
Matty's uncle wanted to see her married to Dirk Reasoner, but Matty knew something her uncle didn't — and that was why Dirk would never trust and respect her, let alone love her . . .

ACROSS THE GREAT DIVIDE *by Kerry Allyne*
It was Jerome whom Nicole loved — so why was it the annoying Lang Jamieson who occupied so much of her thoughts?

FLAME OF DIABLO *by Sara Craven*
Vitas de Mendoza agreed to help Rachel find her brother — but at a price. Would she find the price too high? Or would she pay — far too willingly?

BLUE LOTUS *by Margaret Way*
Susan was rescued from the rain forest of Queensland by Devin Chandler and taken to recover at his cattle station — a private kingdom where the king made his own laws . . .

FRUSTRATION *by Charlotte Lamb*
Considering the tumultuous circumstances of their first meeting, it was hardly surprising that Jake Lang should despise and dislike Natalie Buchan . . .

A DANGEROUS MAN *by Mary Wibberley*
When Tania met Bryden Kane she realised that he was a dangerous man to know — certainly she could sense the danger to her own heart.

APOLLO'S SEED *by Anne Mather*
Martha had been virtually forced to return to Greece and her husband Dion. But it was clear that his only reason for wanting her was to get their child back.

A MAN TO WATCH *by Jane Donnelly*
To Harriet, Jotham Gaul was nothing but an irritating boor who told her she had nothing but her looks — but why should she care about his opinion?

A CERTAIN SMILE *by Marjorie Lewty*
When Amanda discovered her father, she found herself whisked into a world of wealth, of tycoons, of sophistication — and a world that also contained Blair Craddock . . .

STORMY AFFAIR *by Margaret Mayo*
Who did Hamed Ben Slouma think he was, spoiling Amber's peaceful holiday in Tunisia by whisking her off to his house and announcing that he was going to marry her?

— all that's pleasurable in Romantic Reading!
Available November 1979

191